MW01705564

NAKED IN THE SANCTUARY

PROSE SERIES 71

Canada Council for the Arts
Conseil des Arts du Canada

Canada

ONTARIO ARTS COUNCIL
CONSEIL DES ARTS DE L'ONTARIO

Guernica Editions Inc. acknowledges the support of The Canada Council for the Arts.
Guernica Editions Inc. acknowledges the support of the Ontario Arts Council.
Guernica Editions Inc. acknowledges the financial support of the Government of Canada through the Book Publishing Industry Development Program (BPIDP).

JULIE ROORDA

NAKED IN THE SANCTUARY

For Gay,
Thanks for your
encouragement and
support. With love,
Julie Roorda
Oct 12, 2004

GUERNICA

TORONTO – BUFFALO – CHICAGO – LANCASTER (U.K.)
2004

Copyright © 2004, by Julie Roorda and Guernica Editions Inc.
All rights reserved. The use of any part of this publication, reproduced, transmitted in any form or by any means, electronic, mechanical, photocopying, recording or otherwise stored in a retrieval system, without the prior consent of the publisher is an infringement of the copyright law.

Antonio D'Alfonso, editor
Guernica Editions Inc.
P.O. Box 117, Station P, Toronto (ON), Canada M5S 2S6
2250 Military Road, Tonawanda, N.Y. 14150-6000 U.S.A.

Distributors:
University of Toronto Press Distribution,
5201 Dufferin Street, Toronto, (ON), Canada M3H 5T8

Gazelle Book Services, White Cross Mills, High Town, Lancaster LA1 IXS U.K.

Independent Publishers Group,
814 N. Franklin Street, Chicago, Il. 60610 U.S.A.

First edition.
Printed in Canada.

Typeset by Selina.
Printed in Canada.
First edition.

Legal Deposit – Second Quarter
National Library of Canada
Library of Congress Catalog Card Number: 2004100327

National Library of Canada Cataloguing in Publication
Roorda, Julie
Naked in the sanctuary / Julie Roorda.
(Prose series ; 71)
ISBN 1-55071-195-4
I. Title. II. Series.
PS8585.O683N33 2004 C813'.6 C2004-900361-5

CONTENTS

ACKNOWLEDGEMENTS

The author wishes to thank Doug, Nancy, Dan and Jackie Roorda, Michele Milan, Austin Clarke, Steve Lavender, Martin and Deborah McKneally, Antonio D'Alfonso, Halli Villegas, and everyone at *Pagitica*.

Some of these stories have appeared in slightly different form in *McGill Street Magazine, The Fiddlehead, Room of One's Own, Front & Centre Magazine* and *Zygote*.

For Kimberly, Lindsay and Joey

ADVENT

Dagmar is eighty and has been exploring the boundaries of her existence. Most just say she is senile. No one knows how she finds her way in to her neighbours' bedroom, but when the Huisman's awake to the heart-stopping sight of a strange figure in the dark, Dagmar nearly does not make it out. Mr. Huisman pulls a gun from a bedside drawer and aims at the shadow. When his wife flicks on the light, his adrenaline fizzles reluctantly away. You have to pity the old woman, he thinks. She lived there for nearly fifty years before her children concluded she could no longer live on her own and moved her to her youngest daughter's home half a block away. They sold the big white house to the Huisman's, a family they knew from church. Luckily, Mr. Huisman calls Dagmar's family, not the police. At four in the morning of the day before Christmas, they search her person to see if she still has a key, and find nothing.

Black-eyed Lucy is four and cannot tell the difference between her sleeping and waking lives. On the very night her grandmother is terrorizing the neighbours with the stealth of a cat-burglar, Lucy is ice-skating on a marvelous pond with the little blonde girl who is her best friend. She skates fast and strong, executing breath-taking twirls and matching step by intricate step her friend's lilting waltz. The excursion leaves her dazzled and starry on Christmas Eve morning, when the rest of her family is cranky and sag-eyed for having spent half the night up.

Lucy will recount these adventures when her weekly

visits to a child psychologist resume in January. The psychologist is preparing her for kindergarten registration, where her family fears she will be gravely misunderstood if not coached properly beforehand. But Lucy will insist she can indeed spin and dance on the ice, and her mother will elicit a dark-browed frown from the child when she explains, "It was only a dream," as she has so many times before.

Peg is fourteen and for several weeks now, as if in anticipation of the festive season, a circlet of shorting electrical flashes has hung around her head like a halo of rickety dollar-store tinsel. She cannot see straight, stumbling blearily down to breakfast, blinking at the Christmas tree lights which Lucy has turned on. It's a drag, she thinks, having Christmas on Monday. It means she will have to go to church two mornings in a row, when she desperately wants to sleep in. What was all that noisy commotion last night?

Her toast has a greenish tint that makes her stomach flop. Everything appears strange lately. Her parents are so ugly, their faces twisting into gargoyles whenever they speak. And her grandmother, well, she avoids looking at Dagmar at all because whenever she tries, she sees double, a slightly transparent version stepping ahead of Dagmar's body. Her brother Josh has become a hideous, snarling gremlin, and Lucy a slippery imp who eludes her grasp when she steals a slice from her plate. She fears she is losing her sanity.

Bill is forty and concerned for the welfare of his reckless family. After church he plans to speak to his friend, who runs a hardware store, about inside locks that will prevent his mother-in-law from escaping the house without his approval. It is for her own good, her own safety, and frankly, he will sleep better at night knowing his daughter Peg cannot do anything drastic, at least not without the confines of the house. Lucy is so odd and flighty, and even his wife has that nervous pacing streak. Only Josh is really solid. Mud-tracking, snowball-throwing, noisy and brash, his behaviour is at least predictable, for a nine-year-old boy. Yes, the whole family will benefit from some added security.

He would like to strengthen the house from the outside as well. There have been several break-ins in the neighbourhood recently, and an atmosphere of unease that has people sleeping with their weapons. He will reinforce all the locks, put bars on the basement windows. In the meantime, there are tricks, extra precautions which can be taken. He stops his family just outside the door. "Everyone turn around and walk backwards!" he instructs. With all that fresh snow it would be obvious to a potential burglar that the house had just been vacated. "We'll make it look like people have just gone inside."

They form a bizarre procession. Bill steps carefully, clearly defining each misleading print. Peg sinks her face into her scratchy scarf with embarrassment. A memory sparks through her mind of her now dead grandfather with an eight millimetre camera, filming her in the snow, then projecting the films backwards. "How come I don't bump into everything?" she asked. "You must have eyes on the back of your head," he would explained. But she could never find them, underneath her fuzzy red hair.

Josh jumps and hoots, hurling snowballs against the stucco, and attracting every burglar in the area with his racket. His mother pleads in vain for him to hush. Dagmar stops and stares at the strange pattern they have left. As if a whole batch of ghostly visitors has herded up the driveway and disappeared into another dimension. Lucy giggles at the image of the house flapping its doors and lights, rocking with an unsanctioned party while the family is at church.

But they cannot stop. "Don't turn around until we join some other tracks on the sidewalk, otherwise it will look suspicious," Bill says. They are halfway to church before they find some.

Mae is also forty and weary with holding everything together. She surveys the faces of her family settling into their usual pew. Everyone looks sleepy and pale from the interrupted night. She could have left her mother home with the kids to sleep in, but she is not quite sure she can trust any of them anymore. And it is reassuring to the congregation, which no doubt is already buzzing with the news of her mother's midnight travels, to see the whole family there, as though the incident was unimportant.

Josh is wiffling noisily, knocking the back of the pew in front of them. Peg is covering her palms with minuscule script, writing who-knows-what and getting ink stains on her skirt. Bill closes his eyes just a little too long for church protocol. Now Dagmar and Lucy are both staring uncannily at the empty white arch of the sanctuary ceiling, as though they see something. Mae sighs at the harried flutter in her stomach.

This is Lucy's favourite part of December church services, the lighting of the Advent wreath. She likes their varying heights, the first candle the shortest for having burned already three Sundays. Then the others each a light step up to the fourth which is being lit for the first time. Only the tall red one in the centre will be left for tomorrow, Christmas. Lucy shivers with excitement. Somewhere an icy draft seeps in, agitating the candle flames so that they burn quickly, smokily, dangerously close to the evergreen branches decorating the base. Lucy stares, entranced as the wiggly space above the flames expands throughout the church, altering faces and eyes.

By the end of the sermon, the entire congregation is absorbed in the tiny fire drama, and when a spark finally lands on green and sends up a pungent stream of piney smoke, there is a collective gasp. Several men jump forward to slap the sparks out. Only then does Lucy blink and shake strings of hair from her eyes. "We'll have to trim that before tomorrow," her mother whispers to the side of her head.

That afternoon is not the usual quiet of Sunday after church. Peg turns her music up loudly in her bedroom to try and drown out the buzzing in her head. Josh tears through the house, hyper with anticipation of the toy weapons he knows will appear under the tree. The whine of Bill's drill grates against everyone's eardrums as he puts inside locks on the front and back doors, and Lucy howls in protest at being set up on the kitchen stool to have her hair cut.

Dagmar hovers, collecting the shorn strands of Lucy's browny-red hair and telling her old Norwegian stories to distract her attention from the scissors at the corners of her eyes. One story is about a princess whose soul was not inside her body. It was hidden in a seed, inside an apple, on a tree, in a far-off valley, covered from sight by a rosy sunset mist. In order to win her heart, the prince had to find this seed and swallow it.

"Did he find it?" Lucy asks.

"I don't remember," Dagmar says, catching the last of Lucy's hair as her mother lifts her down. She disappears into the living room while Mae blows the itchiness from

Lucy's neck and shakes out the towel that was draped around her shoulders. A few seconds later, an acrid burning smell fills the house. Everyone rushes to the living room to find Dagmar sprinkling Lucy's hair in the fireplace which was lit in a feeble attempt to create holiday cheer.

"Mother! What are you doing?" Mae asks.

"My grandmother always burned hair cuttings," Dagmar says.

"Superstitious," Bill says with disgust and returns to his drill.

"It stinks," Josh says, now holding his nose instead of an imaginary gun.

"Nail clippings too," Dagmar adds, smiling at Peg who has emerged from her room gnawing a finger, leaving ink smudges on her lips.

"That's gross," Peg mutters and leaves again.

"Nothing like a smell to bring the past to life," Dagmar sighs. Lucy wrinkles her nose. They are the only ones by the fire now. Dagmar pulls a sprig of green from the mantle and holds it above the freshly shorn pixie head. "Mistletoe is magic," she says, and pecks Lucy on the cheek.

Dagmar's grandmother is long dead and very wise. She was the one true-blooded Norwegian who married into the Dutch family. That family did not think much of her tales and cures, her magical ministrations. None but her granddaughter Dagmar, who bears her name, cared to listen.

She is huge now, expanded far beyond the limits of her former consciousness. Still, occasionally, she misses some aspect of that sentient life, the smells, the swishiness of skating on the silvery pond when she was just a child. When the family gathers quaintly around the fire to open presents on Christmas Eve, she cannot resist a peek. She leans her head down, a giant peering in her doll house. The others hear only another wintry gust against the window, but Dagmar turns to see her grandmother's gigantic lashes sweep snowflakes from the pane. She exclaims with every phrase of Norwegian her grandmother taught her. Lucy points and waves and giggles with delight at the miraculous sight. But Lucy's parents do not think it is so wonderful. They shift uncomfortably, careful not to catch the other's eye, both silently alarmed. The child seems to be catching her grandmother's senility. Something will have to be done.

Bill finds it reassuring to secure his new locks and hang the keys on a string around his neck. So reassuring that he puts his thirty-eight back in its safety box, and moves this from his bedside table to a dresser across the room. Josh traces his father's footsteps by ear, listening through the air vent. He has never yet dared to touch his father's gun unsupervised, but he always keeps track of where it is hidden just in case the opportunity arises. With snow falling idyllically outside, the family settles, safe and warm on this coziest of winter nights.

The snow stops shortly after midnight and a brisk, but not terribly icy wind clears the sky of clouds. Dagmar and Lucy are delighted to have a wide clear moon to light their way. They weave designs in the fresh snow, and tread a circle of prints around the entire house, walking backward and forward and backward again. "This'll fool any burglar," Lucy says. Her grandmother smiles, but her quieter example cannot mute Lucy's youthful exuberance, and soon, inevitably, someone hears her giggle.

Dagmar can sense the rumble in the house as Bill curses himself for having moved the gun, and again for the trouble unlocking the door. He stops at the sight of his daughter and mother-in-law waving angels in the snow, though the rage keeps coursing through his neck having nowhere to go.

"You'll get pneumonia!" Mae wails, pushing past to snatch up Lucy, whose flannelette pajamas are soaked, her feet red from the snow pushing in the tops of her hastily slipped on snowmobile boots. Mae pulls the two escapees into the house and warm baths despite their insistence that they are not cold. Dagmar returns to her room, shrugging off all reproaches. Shiny-faced Lucy falls swiftly asleep on the couch, but her parents pace the house until morning, drumming up solutions.

Mae is too tired to care what the congregation thinks this time. She keeps her mother and daughter home under close watch, while the others go to church. Strangely, she seems to be the only one catching a cold. She sniffles frequently while stuffing the turkey, preparing all trimmings despite her bad night, for her siblings and their families who will arrive after church. There must be turkey, even if this Christmas turns into a stern family conference.

Lucy emerges from the couch well-rested and ready for breakfast. Her mother sits beside her, holding up her oily, poultry-seasoned hands. "Lucy," she says, trying to appear soft and concerned. "How did you get outside last night?"

Lucy blinks. "I dreamed it," she says. She tips her cereal bowl up to drain the last of the milk, then joins her grandmother who is putting an old record on the turntable. "Please have snow, and mistletoe . . ." Dagmar and Lucy dance around the living room, winking at each other's eyes.

When the church service is over and the savour of

turkey is sifting through the house, people start to arrive. Dagmar stands by the drafty door, despite Mae's protests, and greets each of her children and grandchildren carefully, thoroughly. Then she sits in the living room with all the young ones who are ready to raise a festive racket. Their parents slip into the dining room for a closed conference, armed with names, phone numbers and an un-Christmassy sense of duty. Bill avoids his mother-in-law as he closes the door behind him. He has already decided one thing, that Dagmar will not remain in his house for another night.

Dagmar's suitcase is full and ready beside her bed. She recognized that look in her son-in-law's eyes, the fear of a forty-year-old man who is losing control, unable to predict and protect. She packed early so she can relax and watch her grandchildren.

Peg knows something is going on in her house and in her own head. When she woke this morning there was a pair of shears in her hand and an oddly symmetrical shape cut out from her sheet. She had been dreaming she was making snowflakes to decorate the windows, her favourite craft from her worry free childhood. But with the scrap of cloth in her hand, that peace shifted to embarrassed fear of being found out. She scrunched the sheet up in a ball in her closet. Now, as she seats herself as near to the dining room as she can without being obvious, she experiences a blurry sense of both wanting to know, and reluctance to take part in their adult responsibility. For a second she looks to her smaller siblings and cousins with longing, but decides she must stay, eavesdropping on adulthood.

"I can fly," Lucy tells her rapt cousins. "Last night I flew all the way around the world." The smells from the kitchen lull Dagmar, and after a while she begins to float away. She does not notice that Lucy is dragging furniture around the room.

When three-year-old Darren hits the floor with a crash and a wail, all the adults stampede. Lucy is kneeling on top of a stool which stands atop a box, itself atop the coffee table, six feet up, as high as the angel crowning the Christmas tree. She has just given her cousin a helpful boost to unloose his wings. Before she can loose her own, her father plucks her down with a smack on the bum.

"Mother! What are you thinking, letting them do this?" Mae is aghast.

Dagmar, from the window where she has just glimpsed her grandmother's laced-up boots making enormous tracks in the snow replies, "Let them fly." The siblings exchange significant glances like a round of toasts. Now they are all in agreement.

After Christmas dinner is served and the dishes cleaned, Dagmar's children explain to Dagmar that she must go to a hospital that evening for observation. "It's for your own safety," they say. "We can't protect you properly here."

They are expecting a fight, but Dagmar fetches her bag and hums merrily as she waits for Bill to warm up the car. She hums as she kisses Lucy and all her grandchildren good-bye. They move out to the porch to watch as she settles into the back seat. She rolls down the window and waves, singing as they pull away, "Please have snow, and mistletoe . . ."

Dagmar has been living in her body for many, many years. She sees no reason to continue within the strict and sterile confines of a carefully guarded hospital room, so she stops. Before the year turns, she joins her ballooning grandmother to watch her family enter the funeral home.

Bill and Mae and the other siblings are dark, shrouded by their own blinding guilt and regret. Poor Peg looks fuzzy and miserable, her brother frowning and unruly. But Lucy approaches the coffin with clear, quiet eyes. Many of the flowers and arrangements have a muted Christmassy theme, the florists having used up leftover bits and pieces. Lucy hunts among them for several minutes, finally plucking her chosen piece of greenery. She dangles the mistletoe above her grandmother's old face, and pecks her cheek, before laying the sprig in her hands to rest.

SACRED SEED

The freezer was half full of what appeared to be rows of frothy white beakers. I crammed in the Tupperware container of leftovers and slammed the door.

"What is that?" I wailed. "The white stuff in those . . ."

"Popsickle molds," Mom said. "It's chicken stock. I found that each mold was just the right amount to defrost at one time."

I opened the freezer again to confirm, and when I did, the container I had pushed in carelessly slipped to the floor, opened and splattered lukewarm supper everywhere.

"Clumsy." Mom shook her head.

I crouched down to mop up the mess, glad to have the opportunity to hide my face. She was right, they were popsickle molds full of chicken stock. But they did not erase the image of what I thought I had seen in that instant when I first opened the door – beakers of my dead brother's semen. It was ludicrous. Of course the samples were not here in my parents' refrigerator. They were being kept, at some cost, in a fertility clinic downtown. But after all I had heard that evening, I could hardly blame myself for the mistake.

Sunday family dinner had begun as it always did. My brother Neil jammed his chair back against the wall when the rest of us folded our hands for grace. He twiddled a cigarette over his knuckles to make it clear he was not taking part in, nor condoning the prayer.

Mom served out each plate and handed them around the table. Creamed corn, mashed potatoes, baked fish with white sauce. For several minutes we ate in silence, appreciatively. Then out of the blue, Mom spoke. "We won our case." I could tell this was something important by the way my dad kept eating.

"What case?" I asked.

"We won control of Ben's semen samples," she said.

My cheeks pinkened. I had a hard time looking at my food, let alone continuing to eat.

Mom continued, "Our lawyer . . ."

"Lawyer?" Neil interrupted. "You have a lawyer?"

"Yes. He straightened things out and made it clear that the clinic did not have the right to use it."

"What was the clinic going to use it for?" I asked.

"They weren't going to use it," Mom said. She looked confused. "We want to."

Neil started to laugh, and I too, glancing back and forth between my cooling plate and my mother's ready-to-bloom amaryllis absurdly phallic on the windowsill. My father reached for seconds.

"What's so funny? Ben didn't have the opportunity to have kids. If we find the right person . . . our grandchildren, you know."

Neil kept laughing, but I stopped. A ring of dominoes had just been tipped off and were falling sequentially, racing toward the point of understanding.

"You're going to find a surrogate," I said.

"Not just a surrogate, a real mother. Someone who would let us be involved in the child's life," Mom explained.

"Do you think Ben would have wanted this?" I asked.

"I know Ben wanted children."

"So what are you going to do?" Neil said, spitting white sauce. "Put an ad in the personals?"

My father wiped his mouth with a napkin and got up. He went into the living room and returned with the day's newspaper. He opened it to an ad that had been carefully highlighted, and set it in front of us.

Wanted: Healthy woman who'd like to mother our grandchildren. Sperm from promising young man whose life was cut short. It may be our only chance to give all the love we have.

Ping! The final domino hit the floor. That was it, I thought, their only chance. Unmarried, thirty-five year old daughter and disturbed younger son aside, their only chance.

Neil stood and walked out, his laughter loud and erratic, like a superball bouncing out of control into the street, into traffic. I realized too late that he had the keys to my car.

*

Dad gave me a silent lift home, but did not get out of the car. Smoke was seeping out from under my door and inside Neil lay camped on my couch again, cosying a bottle of Scotch and chain-smoking.

"Join me, I'm celebrating," he said. "Going to be an uncle."

I growled at him and shut myself in my bedroom instead. Part of me wanted to join him, the same part that almost ran after him when he took off with my car. But I had to work in the morning.

I slept badly and was late for my first client anyway. Mr. Cummings. I would have to rub his ears extra long to placate him. If he had it his way, I would be massaging his ears the whole sixty minutes and forget about the arthritis cricking every joint in his back. They are huge, like cabbage leaves in my hands. And when I do massage them, he inevitably falls into a trance-like sleep. Once again, I had to call my partner Jane to help me wake him.

Jane raised her eyebrows at my sleepless face. "Another family dinner, eh?"

I took one of Mr. Cummings' hands and shook it gently. Jane was never so subtle. She slapped his cheeks rapidly back and forth. When that did not work, she hauled his eighty pound frame into a seated position and called into his cabbage ears, "Fire!" We waited in the hall while he dressed, timing him because he has a tendency to climb back on the table and go back to sleep.

"You coming to my party tomorrow?" Jane asked. "There'll be someone there I think you should meet." Jane is always trying to fix me up, and the description of my intended is always the same. He would be good experience for you. What she means is, slightly dangerous. She ran away from home when she was fifteen and lived on the streets for three years, an episode of her life which she describes as *excellent experience*. She thinks I am coddled and naïve. If I only had some *experience* under my belt, I would make great strides in life. Her opinion of pain certainly distinguishes her as a massage therapist. Her clients complain about her roughness, yet they always come back. I, on the other hand, am recommended for the gentle massage.

My parents were not exactly enthusiastic about my choice of career. In fact, they were repulsed, as if massage therapy were little more than prostitution. Prostitution for big, ugly women. But I always figured it was the best way to use my oversized hands, the only way. And although disgusted, I don't think they were surprised. They had always been appalled by my size. Twelve pounds at birth, six feet tall at fifteen. "I don't know where you get it," Mom loved to say. It was pretty clear to me, since my dad is six foot five. But in our family, the genes attached themselves to the wrong sex. Only my brothers inherited my mother's bird bones.

"Hmmmm," I responded non-commitally. Mr. Cummings opened the door. He was awake and dressed, although his sweater was on backwards. I ushered him out, happy to escape Jane's narrowing gaze.

I could not decide which would be worse, Jane's continuing to try and set me up, or her giving up. Mom gave up when I turned thirty, and there were only a few real attempts before that, because her first and overriding criterion was that he be taller than me. The truth is, her candidates were never all that bad. One of them, in fact, a lanky classics professor named Ron was quite nice. I stopped calling him when I realized how well we were hitting it off. I could not politely refuse to go out with someone my mother had recommended, but I could certainly refuse to fall in love.

*

I was a little apprehensive about going back to my parents' house after my last client, but I needed to do my laundry, and the prospect of the filthy laundry room in my apartment building was much worse than anything they could say. I knocked and opened the door without waiting, as I always do. My parents sat at the dining table, heads locked over a pad of paper.

"What are you two conspiring about?"

"We're preparing a questionnaire for applicants," my mother said.

I retreated to the laundry room, leaving the door open so I could hear what they said.

"Do we want to specify denomination?" my father asked.

"We can't be too picky. As long as she's not Catholic."

"What about Mormon? Or Jehovah's Witness?"

"Mormon? That's not even Christian, is it? I think that's a cult. And not Jehovah's Witness, that would be worse." Consternation circled my mother's head like crows. "Maybe we should be more flexible on Catholic."

"I think we have a good chance sticking with our own type churches. We could make a list. Let's see, there are the Baptists, United – a bit free thinking, but we might need someone freethinking!" My father chuckled, and Mom joined him giggling.

Ben was the only one of us three siblings who continued to go to church as an adult. Neil and I preferred to make fun of their little church feuds, the Presbyterian clannishness, behind their backs. I would have to tell Neil about their newly widening horizons.

"Methodist," my father said. "What about Pentecostal?"

"I don't know, they're awfully loud, aren't they?"

I turned on the washing machine and slipped out the back door.

*

Ben was a brilliant biochemist. He taught at the university, and was always working on some important new research project. Pleasant, good-looking, and well on his way to the standard paraphernalia of success my parents could relate to. They had no doubt that if he had lived past thirty he would have married, had kids and a house. Even after the cancer diagnosis, he seemed to do everything he could to remain on that course. The semen samples were collected in case the radiation therapy left him sterile. The only thing that ever got in his way was his untimely death. Now it seemed that even the problem of death could be overcome, if my parents had their way. They would get him back on the right track. I wondered what Ben would think of the whole scheme if he knew of it. Then again, maybe he did know, maybe it was all his doing, continuing his biochemical experiments from beyond, the whole earth his laboratory, his family a bit of sludge on a glass slide. I was startled by the image of myself under a microscope, looking up at a sky that was just a big tunnel to Ben's grotesquely magnified eye, watching, winking. He was about to inject a bit of himself back into the world below, about to get a second chance.

*

I had been walking for an hour when I returned to the house. There was a strange car in the driveway, and a strange woman, about forty years old, all matching in a mauve suit, sitting on the couch, opposite my parents. All three looked startled when I walked in, the woman's purple mouth became a perfect O.

"We thought you'd gone," my mother said accusingly.

"I've still got a load for the dryer." I nodded to the woman, then stopped short, when I realized what was happening. I had walked in on an interview. The woman looked confused.

"This is Teresa, our daughter," my mother said.

"Your daughter?" the woman asked sharply, clearly wanting an explanation.

"Yes. She's . . . thirty-five," Mom said, as if that was one. "We also have another son, Neil. He has a personality disorder."

Personality disorder? Where had they come up with that term? They had begun sending Neil to psychiatrists and psychologists and counselors when he was nine years old, after he had sung his own, slightly obscene lyrics to the tune of "Faith of Our Fathers" to some of their friends during after-church coffee. He went from one specialist to another, changing every few months. My parents were never satisfied with the diagnosis, because the diagnosis was always the same: there was nothing wrong with him. He was intelligent, and clear-thinking, and his choices were his own.

My parents' frustration escalated throughout his teens, and finally peaked on a memorable Sunday night when eighteen-year-old Neil announced that he was going to move in with Carol, a thirty-two-year-old woman who spent her days making sculptures from old dolls, broken furniture and yards and yards of telephone wire. "Sorry, Ma," Neil had said as he opened the front door. "Guess there's just no accounting for bad taste."

The mauve woman gathered up her coat and bag and left. My mother turned on me. "Are you going to chase them all away like that?"

"You had to tell her about us sometime," I said. "And I don't get it. That woman is at least as old as I am." I pulled my clothes out of the washer and stuffed them into my bag still wet.

"Well, you can't have Ben's baby, can you?" she snapped.

"Aaaachh!" Why did she have to say that? What a thought – incestuous bodily fluids mingling in a beaker. But would the term incest apply in a laboratory? I tried to think of something that would disgust them back. "Isn't it wrong for an unmarried woman to have Ben's baby? Isn't that adultery?" I said sarcastically, but my father failed to catch my tone.

"Of course not," he said. "Artificial insemination is not adultery. It's not adultery if there's no pleasure."

*

"Does that make it an immaculate conception?" I related the entire episode to Neil while hanging my wet clothes on every available space in my apartment, though I knew it would make everything smell like his cigarettes.

"Heavens, no. This will not be a Catholic baby," Neil said. "Besides, I think there likely was some pleasure involved. There's nothing high-tech about donating sperm. Just some magazines and a little white cup."

"How do you know?"

"Fifty bucks a spurt, no taxes. If you can muster enough strength for a few rounds a week, it's a pretty good living," he said.

I stared at him. "Do you mean to say – they might already have dozens of grandchildren somewhere!"

"Yeah," he laughed and pounded at a lit match he'd dropped among his clothing.

*

After several weeks, the search for a candidate was not going well. We got an update each Sunday.

"Most of these ladies just want money," Dad said.

"Either that or they're obviously unsuitable," said Mom.

Neil laughed. "It's nice to hear that other people's children are imperfect as well."

This was too much for Mom and she started crying into her meatloaf. I felt guilty. I was cheered by their failure, but if their plan was doomed anyway, it could not hurt to be more supportive. "We could go shopping and get you a new interview outfit," I suggested. "That would make you feel more confident." I regretted the words as soon as they were out. How many times had my mother said that very thing to me over the last several years? The insulting implication always that I should be looking for a real career.

However, Mom perked visibly. "Saturday! We'll go this Saturday."

Neil rolled his eyes at me. He never indulges in guilt.

*

As soon as we arrived at the crowded mall, Mom began a steady stream of suggestions concerning my wardrobe. "Look at these cream blouses, they're on sale! You should get yourself a couple. Cream blouses are always useful." She tried on several herself. They all looked the same to me, but she hmmmed and hawed over each one in front of the mirror.

Shopping with Mom was always torturous. When I was a child, shopping for school clothes, she would send me to the dressing room with arms full of items I knew were too small. I would try the first, and it would not budge over my bum. "It's too small," I would call but she would insist that I keep trying. On and on, until finally she would give in and hand the proper size over the door.

"You can't possibly be into a size fourteen already," she would say. "It's ridiculous."

After several more stores and blouses, my jaw was aching from gritting my teeth. "Mom," I said. "I'll buy you an ice cream cone. Wait here."

She sat on a mall bench. When I returned with the ice cream she was staring at the crowds with a spacy expression.

"She's pretty, isn't she?" she said.

"What?" I asked.

She gestured with her cone toward a teeny, smartly-suited woman standing in line for freshly squeezed orange juice. The woman kept lifting her evenly polished nails to smooth her careful, shoulder-length hair which had not a strand out of place.

"Sure," I said slowly. And there I was, sitting in the mall with my mother, watching girls. "What about her?" I pointed to the tall woman vigorously shaking the orange juice behind the stand. My mother grimaced.

For every mouse-like woman my mother pointed to, I deliberately picked someone big, lumbering, a little unruly. Like me. A statuesque woman with electric orange hair and miraculous heels tromped by.

"You know," I said. "Ben had a thing for redheads."

"Really!" Mom jumped on this and surveyed the crowd with renewed vigour. The Amazon had disappeared.

It was not a lie; it was a secret. Her name was Ginger. I never met her, and I did not actually know that she was Amazonian in stature. I only knew that Ben had described her as "red-haired and larger than life," and being of more than average size myself, I idealized her as such. She was a gas bar attendant from Thunder Bay, and I was never very clear on the details of their meeting, except that she was in Toronto visiting her sister at the time. She extended her stay for two weeks – two weeks spent hiding at Ben's place – before he drove her home. He did not tell me anything about her until he returned, skulked back into Toronto and rang my doorbell at three in the morning.

Four days earlier I had come home from work to find my car was missing from its regular parking spot. I could not believe it had been stolen, not just because it was a worthless, falling-apart clunker. I just had a feeling that I should not tell anyone. The next day my mother phoned.

"Do you know where Ben is?" she asked. "He wasn't home last night, and today neither."

It was several minutes before I made a conscious connection, but I felt compelled to cover for him anyway. "Didn't he have that conference in Windsor or something?" I said.

"I thought that was next month."

"Maybe, but there was something . . ."

"Are you sure?"

"You know those biochemistry things he goes to," I said.

"It's just that he's been acting odd lately," she said.

I had not noticed anything odd, but she would consider it alarming that she was not up to date on every detail of Ben's life. When I finally got my mother off the phone, I checked the kitchen drawer for my spare car keys. Gone. Ben had a key to my apartment.

I waited and found myself digging pits full of fibs to explain both absences. I was almost to the breaking point when I awoke to my buzzer, and I knew it was Ben. He did not say anything. He just shrugged and held out my car keys. I gestured him in and he collapsed on the couch. He looked like he had not slept for a week.

"Don't tell Mom, will you?" he said finally.

"What's there to tell?"

That is when he told me that she was larger than life, that they had been wildly in love for a month, that he had driven her home so that she would not be stuck in Toronto after he told her that he wanted to break up.

I stared at him. My eyes felt like foreign objects wedged into my face. "You drove my car to Thunder Bay and back?"

"Back in one piece," he said. "And there's a full tank of gas in it."

"Why did you break up with her if you were in love?"

He shook his head. "It would never have worked. She was too different, too weird. She would never have fit in."

Fit in with who, I wondered, but I did not ask. He had already made his choice and acted upon it. And he had driven all the way back from Thunder Bay, after the break-up without encountering the second thought that might have turned him back. He started slouching back into the couch, and his eyes were drooping, so I left him there, and when I got up in the morning, he was gone. Three weeks later, he was diagnosed with cancer.

*

My mother phoned Thursday morning before work. "You're coming early on Sunday for Easter." There was a particular excitement in her voice that made me suspicious. Easters were dreadful. Mom always made hard-boiled eggs, carefully painted them babyish pinks and blues, then served them with coffee after church. They reminded me of the way my breasts felt when I was twelve, sprouting and painfully tight in the too-small satiny bras she insisted on. One year I finally said to her, "Just because the eggs are coloured, doesn't mean they're dessert."

She glared at me so savagely that I took one anyway. The pale green dye had leached through into the white of the egg. It made me nauseous. I tried to retreat to my room.

"Where do you think you're going, young lady? You think just because you're wearing a bra now you don't have to spend time with the family?" That was always a big thing for her. Holidays were spent together in the living room, no matter how miserable everyone was. I sat back down and lengthened the ladders in my nylons. Mom cross-stitched, Dad read the newspaper, Neil huddled under an afghan, absorbed in its pattern. Only Ben was content, working on a cross-word puzzle.

Suddenly, my mother jumped up, dumping eggshells and embroidery. She snatched at Neil's afghan. "What are you doing? You've ruined it!" Neil had found a loose end and methodically unraveled nearly a third. The kinky yarn straggled across the room like strewn intestines. She ran to her bedroom, breaking her own taboo. Only Ben could coax her out later by suggesting a game of Trivial Pursuit.

Despite my apprehension, I assured her I would arrive on time. I hung up and left for work. It had become a habit to check the newspaper delivered to our waiting room each day for my parent's ad. But for the first time, it was not there. I panicked and started flipping pages. Maybe they had changed the wording and it came somewhere else alphabetically. Maybe they had switched dailies. It was not there. Jane found me in this fluster.

"Are you coming to my party Sunday?" she demanded.

"Easter? I can't, family."

She glared and shook her head. "You'll never meet anyone, you know that?"

I did not care that she was angry. All I could think about was that they were no longer running the ad. It could only mean one thing. When I arrived home, Neil had built an immense pyramid of cigarette butts in the middle of the coffee table. I snarled at him. "They've found somebody." He did not respond. "You know, it's becoming increasingly obvious why they've given up on you!" With a sheet of newspaper, I swept the pile of butts out from under his unsteady hand.

"They've given up on you too, babe," he said.

"I could still have a baby!"

Neil laughed then adopted the psychiatrist's tone he had perfected at thirteen. "You spend half your energy secretly rebelling against them, and the other half back-tracking to try and please them. But you won't actually move either way. You know what that's called? It's called passive aggression."

I wished I knew some label to throw at him, but I had not the benefit of all his psychiatric training. All I could think of was "personality disorder." "You spend all your energy wallowing in your own destruction!" I said.

Neil laughed. "At least I'm not a hypocrite."

I went to my bedroom and shut the door, just catching myself from slamming it because it seemed too ridiculous to be thirty-five and stomping to my room in my own apartment. It was all ridiculous and Neil was right. I did not want to be my parents' vicarious agent, but I did not want them to stop wanting this. I did not want a baby, but I did not want them to stop wanting me to want one. I was running in two directions and getting nowhere. Ben, on the other hand, had been fully committed to pleasing them. Both of us had given up a possible love; I had dumped Ron, Ben had left Ginger. So why not go along? Live my own life and let them live Ben's. Then I would have to figure out what I really did want.

When I returned to the living room, Neil was gone and he had taken the knapsack which contained all his worldly possessions with him. I opened the window and fanned out the smoky air.

*

The sun was unusually intense for Easter Sunday, heating the back of my neck, like someone watching me. I pulled up behind a strange car in the driveway, and as I did, the front screen door opened a crack and Neil's hand appeared with a lit cigarette, followed by the puffs of smoke he blew outside. I figured he would be there. After all, it was their couch or mine. Mom came rushing to greet me. She was flushed and looked happier than I had seen her in a while. "Teresa, come in. I want you to meet Gina." A red-haired woman in a green dress sat on the couch. She was not an Amazon, but she was bigger than my mother and she had many freckles. She held a turquoise hard-boiled egg in one hand, but seemed unsure what to do with it. She looked over to Neil, who had picked up a pink egg and sat down opposite her, but he, immediately understanding her plight, offered no help. He held his egg up to the light with a look of awe, then proceeded to balance it in the crook of his elbow.

"Gina," I said, as I offered her my hand and prepared to sit down.

She smiled. "Actually, my friends have always called me Ginger."

WEDDING DRESS

Every woman in Rachel's family has made her own wedding dress. Her sister practiced early on her dolls, designing elaborate Victorian frills, while Rachel was content to dress Barbie in Kleenex. Still, for her sixteenth birthday, she received a state-of-the-art sewing machine, and when she announced her engagement, the family rushed her out to look at patterns.

The sewing machine now sits on two milk crates in Rachel's sparse apartment. Nick will be moving in after the wedding at which they hope to acquire some modest furnishings. For now, the expanse of light carpet and bare walls is depressing, and the folds of white fabric across Rachel's knees fit right in. She chose the simplest pattern she could find, but with two months left before the wedding, she is still struggling. Stitching and unstitching, rushing out to buy more fabric to replace the sections she ruins.

The door buzzes and she can hardly stand, her legs are so cramped from kneeling in front of the crates. Apprehensive at the unexpected visitor, she totters over to the button panel.

"Rachel? It's me."

The intercom distorts the voice, but she knows it. Icy fear runs over her scalp. Something must be wrong if her father is in Windsor.

"Dad! What are you doing here?"

"Let me come up. We'll talk."

She releases the lock, then waits. Never has anyone's trip up the elevator taken so long. Her father cannot have driven all the way from Kingston just to chat. She paces, then jumps when he knocks.

"Rachel, I know this is a surprise," he says.

"Something's wrong."

"Well, yes, in a way. Nobody's sick or anything. The truth is . . . there's something I have to confess to you."

Confess! What a monstrous word! It evokes medieval trials and inquisitions, messy confessions of sins. Rachel can't deal with this just yet. She needs something neutral.

"Tea?" she squeaks. He nods and Rachel escapes to the kitchen. She stays to watch the kettle boil, tinging spoons against cups to sound busy. Neither speaks until she returns with the tea and places it on a milk crate-table.

"I have to tell you before you hear from anyone else," he is saying. An alarm goes off in Rachel's head. Other people already know. "I have sinned in a way that has hurt many people, including you and Nick. The truth is, I've had an affair with a woman." He pauses. "Your mother has . . . she is forgiving me. I know this is a terrible thing to do while you're planning your wedding, but I couldn't put off telling you. I'm sorry for that, Rachel. You have a right to be hurt and angry, but I pray that you will come to forgive me."

Rachel's face burns with embarrassment. They do not talk about sex or sin in her family, it is never even alluded to. And this raw discussion of churchy emotions is equally discomfiting. But how can she possibly refuse to forgive him? He has driven seven hours in penitence. Why didn't he just put peas in his shoes?

"I guess . . . we're all human," Rachel says meekly. He

is relieved, she thinks. He was just beginning to think I might rip the family pattern and make a scene. “There’s something else.” He rubs his eyes which are usually so clear and penetrating. Now they look tired and watery. Rachel notices strands of white in his dark hair for the first time. “The woman I was involved with is Marilyn.”

The words “confess” and “adultery” are swirling in Rachel’s head, but she has not imagined a real person. The familiar name is startling.

*

Rachel first heard Marilyn’s name last fall. Her sister and her brother-in-law were busy engaging their church in the business of social activism. At their prompting, her parents also got involved.

“We’re going to have a guest for an indefinite period of time,” her mother said. Her mother is Grace, in name and manner. She speaks flawlessly, certain of her rightness. “She’s had many problems and a history of abusive relationships. Generally a very needy person. She’s started coming to church now, and she’s going to stay here until she gets on her feet.”

Needy person. They repeated that phrase several times. Rachel met Marilyn at Christmas. Her sister told her in hushed tones in the kitchen that there would be no alcohol around this time.

“Marilyn has a history of alcoholism,” Donna whispered. “And you know, once an alcoholic . . . Better to avoid any temptation.”

“I wonder if she’s ever had a real family Christmas like this before,” her mother said.

“Not likely,” Donna responded. She handed Rachel a

bowl of non-alcoholic fruit punch to take into the living room.

Rachel was surprised by Marilyn's composure and attractiveness. There was no sign of the unstable, self-destructive person Rachel expected. Marilyn looked quite elegant in a green embroidered dress. Could she have made it herself? She found herself talking easily with Marilyn about books and school. Nobody had mentioned that Marilyn had gone to art school. She tended to avoid Rachel's mother and sister, but was polite when they tossed her comments like, "Bet you've never had real home-made fruitcake before!"

*

Without finishing his tea, Rachel's dad gets up to leave. "I think it will take time to sort out feelings. So I should go. I'm staying at a hotel tonight, and we can get together tomorrow. In the mean time, you'll want to speak to Nick," he says.

Nick. She is so busy anticipating the relief of being alone, that she has not thought of telling Nick. Her father leaves with no ceremony, and Rachel surveys the room for something to kick. The sewing machine is heavy enough to take the whole force of her foot. It slides off the crate with a satisfying thunk. She tries to dump the dress with the same heave, but it is too light and swishy. It slithers onto the rug.

*

Nick pushes his tongue into his right cheek. His perplexed look. "So what's happened to Marilyn?"

"I don't know. He wasn't saying much about her. I assume she moved out."

They have trouble making love that night. Usually Rachel is inhibited by the worry that her parents will find out. Now they're both dulled by a weary heaviness, and Rachel finds herself lying awake while Nick dozes off. She can't figure out what she is supposed to be feeling besides a vague anger. She tries to imagine how she would feel if Nick were to have an affair, but cannot relate that kind of pain and humiliation to her mother. Grace, who is always above reproach and in control. It seems more like a test which Rachel and her father must pass. The others sit like a jury, benevolently forgiving. And what about Marilyn? A history of needs and abusive relationships. Well, history repeats itself.

*

The phone wakes Rachel the next morning. It's Donna, with her businessy voice. "I guess you know by now. I thought I should call and tell you what's going on here."

"What do you mean?" Usually Rachel tries to sound chipper and pretend they have not got her out of bed. Early rising is an assumed virtue. But she has not slept well, and doesn't care if Donna hears her annoyance.

"We're all praying, of course. There is a lot to deal with. But he has confessed and repented. And we must forgive, because we all sin and because that is Christ's example." She speaks with embarrassing bluntness. "As a community, we must come together in love and support."

"As a community?"

"The church, of course."

So the whole church knows! Rachel should have

guessed. They would not be satisfied with a closed family confession.

*

Her father arrives a few hours later and offers to take her and Nick out for lunch. Rachel does not really want to see him, but he carries on as though it is the right and necessary thing to do. He confirms Donna's words. He confessed to the church council and was stripped of his office of elder. They had entrusted Marilyn to his care, and he had betrayed that, though he does not actually mention Marilyn's name. He focuses on the church, the forgiveness. Rachel's scrambled eggs are too heavy to swallow.

They leave the restaurant and walk along the river. Rachel is careful to put Nick between her father and herself, and avoids discussing wedding details. Eventually the two men start discussing cars and Rachel concentrates on throwing pebbles into the water. A cold wind numbs her hands and shakes the empty trees. They will be grey for several weeks yet. Why won't he just leave? she thinks. He's waiting for something, but I don't have anything to give him.

Finally, they reach his car. She stiffens when he hugs her and backs away from that aftershave and a tinge of sweat that is her father's smell. She is glad when he is gone.

*

Three weeks later, Nick and Rachel travel to Kingston for Easter weekend. Rachel dreads seeing her family all together. When they arrive, it is clear that everything is under control, under the blanket.

"The next time you come it will be for your wedding," her mother says. Rachel tries to detect something different in her greeting, something desperate, an extra tightening, but it is not there. Everyone carries on.

There is a scare at dinner. Donna's husband Robert stands and clears his throat, "I have something to say." For an instant, Rachel freezes, just like she used to at prayer request time in church. Every Sunday, before the interminable congregational prayer, the minister would ask whether there were any additional requests. Members would stand and speak of accidents and sickness. Sometimes people would give requests that were mysterious and anonymous.

"Let us pray for someone in emotional distress."

"Someone has sinned. Let us pray that he will be guided back to God."

It was irrational, but Rachel always feared someone might be alluding to her. She lowered her head to hide her red face, and prayed silently for the requests to end.

"Donna and I are going to have a baby!" Robert continues to noisy exclamations around the table. Her mother beams at her father, reaches over and grabs his knee. He stands for an apple juice toast.

*

The relationship that Rachel's parents have displayed has always been very proud. They knew when to hold hands or arms in a way that was never inappropriate, but a carefully manufactured picture of loving respect. This picture was like other tenets of their religious belief which were sternly upheld as right, like no shopping on Sunday. There were no questions, though Rachel sometimes wondered where the line between reality and religion lay.

On Saturday morning, having been careful to wake early, Rachel stops in the hall beside the kitchen. Her mother is sitting at the table, staring vacantly over her coffee with a tired sadness Rachel has never seen before. When her mother notices her, the look disappears so quickly that she is not sure whether she has imagined it. The controlled superior woman returns.

Seconds later, her sister is at the door with the day's agenda. She scolds Rachel when she learns she has not brought her wedding dress along for inspection.

"You've only got a few more weeks!" Donna says. She and her mother bustle her into a car and hurry around the city speaking to custodians and caterers, eager to finalize all of the wedding plans. Almost as though they know how she is feeling. Bulldozing uncertainty with preparations.

*

Traditionally, Rachel's mother's family gathers after church on Easter. This time at Aunt Ruth's house. The noise is immense. An uncle pounding out hymns on the piano, the odd aunt sings along. Dogs bark and children screech in the midst of countless conversations. Rachel glances at her father from time to time. He is quieter than usual, and speaks carefully and lightly to those who address him. His family sits at intervals around the room. An image fleets through Rachel's mind of secret guards stationed to keep sly eyes on him from every vantage.

Once she walks into the kitchen just in time to hear

Ruth say, "Well, Marilyn was a manipulative woman." She still hasn't learned Marilyn's fate.

"Thank you, Lord, for bringing us together as family, and what a blessing it is," an uncle drones. There are too many people to sit around the table formally, but never too many to be quieted down for a prayer. Rachel bows her head and hopes there will be no embarrassing innuendoes about transgressions.

After dinner, her father stands and holds up a hand. "Donna and Robert have asked me to announce that they are expecting a baby in the fall." Before the scandal, he would have spoken loudly and boisterously. Now he is less certain. The response is not muted though. Everyone jumps to shake his hand or kiss him in a flurry of congratulation. He looks shrunken beneath their heavy-handed forgiveness.

The room is hot and stuffy with so many bodies. Cooking, diapers, dogs and sweat thicken the air. It reminds Rachel of the humid summer when she was twelve. Every year they rented a cottage on a lake near Collingwood. Often they had the same neighbours. For a few years there was a flamboyant black-haired woman who arrived in a yacht with her husband and young son. She was someone to chat with at the little store or on the dock. One afternoon, Rachel's mother prepared to go into town. Her sister was eager to find fabric for a new jumpsuit pattern, but Rachel begged off and joined her father at the dock.

"Can I go fishing with you?"

He looked surprised to see her. "You're not going into town?"

"No. I'd rather go in the boat." He hesitated and looked around. "Well, of course, you can come with me.

Hop in." He moved slowly, but eventually they started out. The day was sticky and so still that the water had a layer of unmoving green slime on its surface. The small motor boat broke through the slime leaving a clear trail from the dock to the place where they stopped to fish. Her dad seemed distracted, but she was busy catching fish, each coated with green from sliding through the surface.

At one point, Rachel looked up and noticed a figure on the dock. Laura, the black-haired woman. Laura stood for a long time looking out before leaving.

Her dad talked about freedom. All the great wilderness there was in Canada and how they should get out and explore it. "Just look at that landscape of trees," he said. "Wonders. All the different shades of green. You can't help but wonder." He was staring at the dock where Laura no longer stood.

On the way back her stomach felt full of the sickly warm algae. And when they returned to the cottage and the enthusiastic welcomes of her sister and mother, the green matter thickened and she felt she had to lie down.

*

"Maybe we shouldn't get married," Rachel says, and Nick nearly swerves off the road. "I mean, maybe we should wait and just live together."

"Are you crazy?" Nick says. His expression is wide and alarmed. "They would freak! Especially after what's happened."

"Or we could elope. Then they couldn't object to us living together."

"But what about all the plans and the money already

spent? They'd be livid. And they'd think it was because of this . . . business with your father. It would make everyone look really bad."

He doesn't ask why she is having second thoughts.

The road back to Windsor seems interminable. Wilderness on both sides is all grey and rocky, with no sign of colour except for the needly evergreen.

"Why would he confess like that?" she finally says. "So publicly."

"He's got a lot to lose," Nick says. "The wedding and now a grandchild. You know, he's really lucky he has a family who wants him to stay."

"But whose decision was it?" For the first time it occurs to Rachel to wonder if maybe her father loved Marilyn.

*

Rachel puts off returning to Kingston until the day before the wedding. Her sister and mother have all the preparations in hand anyway, she just has to show up. Moreover, she does not want them to see the state of her wedding dress until the very end. If they have a chance, they will certainly rally to fix it up. But in her sulky, rebellious state of mind, she doesn't want it fixed and deliberately hides it until the ceremony is an hour away. Still, she feels sheepish when she does finally stand in front of them and sees their faces. Tact quickly covers the aghast ripple.

"I thought there was going to be a bow at the back," her mother says.

"I decided I liked it better without. The simple look," Rachel responds, but she is sure they know she is lying. She feels slightly more mortified than she expected to be.

And looking ahead, she suddenly realizes how many other people will see her in this dress, not just her family. She will have to try and distract them from inspecting messy buttons and uneven seams. There will be an awful lot of experts in the audience.

"You should hold your bouquet a little to the right," Donna suggests. Rachel feels herself turning pink. When she moves the bouquet, she realizes that it hides the crooked darts at her waist.

*

On the way to the church, it occurs to her that Marilyn was originally invited to the wedding. Her sister must have surreptitiously removed Marilyn's name from the seating plan. Or did someone actively un-invite her? Maybe they are all just assuming she will not show up. Perhaps they plan to guard all doors and prevent her from entering. Rachel imagines an ugly scene and finds herself disappointed to think it is unlikely Marilyn would want to try anything. She might not be in Kingston anymore. If anyone knows where she is, they are not saying anything.

Everyone lines up for the procession. Donna stands in front, impeccable in her pink dress. Rachel's mother is on one arm and her father on the other. This is the latest trend in the socially active branch of the church. The whole family gives the bride away. Ironic, when it seems they are closing in on her. Rachel knows she should be concentrating on her feet, but she scans the audience for Marilyn. She's not there. Only the smiles of the people Rachel has known all her life. When the ceremony is over, Rachel does not know whether she has made any mistakes.

The reception blurs. She does not have to think about

what she is doing, because someone is always there to prompt her. Moving is difficult because her dress is too tight around the knees. She feels drunk watching the circle of people whir around her. Every movement looks exaggerated and slow. When her mother puts her hand on Rachel's father's back, it looks like she is giving him a huge push. Then he is standing in front of Rachel for the next dance.

He has taken his glasses off and his eyes are bloodshot. His skin has the shriveled look of peaches that have been in the fridge too long. They are both hot and sweaty and untimely dancers.

"So are you happy, Rachel?" he asks.

The words startle her from her fuzzy vision. "Of course," she mutters. Over his shoulder, they stand in a line. Her mother, her sister and her brother-in-law all smile their approval.

JIZO

I believe we had an agreement. Unspoken, but absorbed, bloodstream to bloodstream. I told you the time was not right, and you acquiesced, finally, after seven months of your persistent presence. But don't think I did not want you. Do not think I don't want you back.

Amy gave you your name. Without you, I would never have met Amy. I sat in a bar with my housemate Helen, drinking soda water and worrying about where I was going to live, about what the second-hand smoke was doing to your developing brain cells and the deafening bass to your fluid-filled ears. When Amy began to sing, I wanted you to hear that voice.

After the set, Helen brought Amy over to our table. I could not hear what they were saying, until Helen leaned towards my ear. "Amy says she's looking for a roommate." Amy slid from her chair to the padded bench beside me. The place was crowded and her thigh below her cut-off jeans touched mine. My loose baby-doll dress still disguised you.

"You're looking for a place for June," Amy said, her voice as astonishing in my ear as when she sang.

"Did she tell you why?" I asked.

Amy shook her head and smiled. "Let's find someplace quieter." The bar had an outside patio. The street was noisy, but we did not have to yell anymore.

"I'm taking next year off from school because I'm pregnant, due in October," I said bluntly.

Amy did not blink. So I continued. "Since I won't be a student, I have to get out of the co-op."

Amy drank directly from her beer bottle, and shook her hair back. She had one of those working-class haircuts, bangs layered around the sides of her face to her ears, straight to her shoulders in the back. Her heavy eyebrows hooded the darkest blue eyes. "I'm only concerned about the summer," she said. "I've got a lease till the end of August, but my roommate just took off for the west coast. Let's say you move in, fulfill the lease, and at the end of the summer, we'll go from there."

It was a perfect solution for me, and I told Amy so. "I don't know what I'll do . . . eventually. The summer will be a good chance to sort things out."

"Great!" Her smile was hypnotizing. "When do you want to check the place out? Tomorrow?"

"Okay," I said, and we stood up to return inside. "If you don't mind living with a water balloon."

Amy put one hand on the small of my back and the other on the growing ball of my stomach. "Not at all," she said. I could have been taken aback by the familiarity of her gesture. Her touch was hot through my thin cotton dress. You must have felt it.

Two weeks later, we sat in our kitchen and Amy put a ring on a string to determine your sex. She held it still in front of you and waited until it began swinging in a circle.

"A girl!" she said.

"What should I name her?"

"I always liked the name Annabel," Amy said. "It's a bit old-fashioned to saddle a child with."

"If only she didn't have to go out into the world," I said. "It would be perfect."

*

I miss that cozy apartment with yellow-wood floors that reflected warm light. It was crowded, hardly bigger than my Tokyo room now. But here in Japan, there are no luminescent lights. Everything is fluorescent, and the dull straw floors do not reflect a thing.

I am seldom home in the evenings anyway. That is when I work, in a hostess bar. I want to have money saved the next time I need it. It is terrible work. Night after night listening to confessions in broken English, pouring him another Scotch with ice, although his face is already as pink as the flesh of a ripe watermelon, eagerly lighting his cigarettes, though he blows smoke in my face. The worst clients are the ones who want to dance. They clutch me close to their sweaty navy suits and ask whether my pubic hair is blonde as well.

Amy and I were delighted when the ring swung full-circle, but sometimes I think that you should come back as a boy. What blasphemy, the idea that you might be reincarnated, and even worse, that you might have a choice. The doctor said your defects began early, in the first couple of months, my hidden thoughts distorting your organs. If you knew you were going to leave, why didn't you leave earlier, before I had to tell my parents?

They wanted to know who your father was, and I told them, "A mistake." Amy got more detail. "Her father is a broken condom." That is not what you want to hear, but it is true. He does not know you exist.

It was a messy, fumbled evening when you were conceived. Afterwards, when I walked the chilly blocks to my co-op room, freezing rain began to fall, slickening the snow-covered ground. I heard the rare rumble of January thunder and knew something was up.

*

On days off, I go to Kamakura, just outside Tokyo. Kamakura is full of temples where there are thousands of small identical statues in rows. The older ones are made of stone, the newer of plastic. Most are clothed with tiny bibs and hats, or just wrapped in scarves. They are surrounded by toys of all sorts. Dolls, jewelry, plastic guns.

"Jizo," a hostess told me. "A Buddhist figure, protector of children. Each statue represents a dead child, mostly miscarriages and abortions."

I am drawn to the Jizos again and again and watch others who visit. Usually women alone tend their own. Once a teenaged girl and her mother picked one out from its row and hauled it down to a temple wall where a garden hose was coiled. They scrubbed the Jizo down with brushes and soap. Whose child? Abortion, miscarriage, or death after birth?

I considered an abortion, but I could not face the prodding of surgical steel. Instead, I tried to talk you out of your life. "Not now," I kept saying. "It's too early." Rain, rain, go away. Come again another day. Maybe it amounts to the same thing, a doctor's tools, or my reluctance to welcome you.

When I wander among the Jizos, I put my hand to my belly where I used to feel your elbows and your limbs. I once read that everything, the entire universe, is inside God. It gave me a remarkable sense of security. Even if I cannot see what you are doing, you could be the right hand, and I the left. Where are you now that you are not safe inside me? If you are in heaven, I am God's miscarriage.

The subject of heaven was always a stumbling block for me and my catechism teachers. Reverend deGelder told us that heaven would be a return to Eden in which we would be perfect again.

"But it can't really be like Eden, I mean, after what we have learned, knowledge of good and evil," I said.

"There will be no knowledge of evil in heaven," he said.

"You mean God will erase our memories?"

"It is not for us to know God's methods. Jesus' blood was shed to remove our guilt, to return us to innocence. It is the only way to be happy," he said.

"But how can we forget all this?" I asked.

"Don't you want to be happy?"

*

We moved in with Amy a week after I met her. The apartment was on the ground floor of a house, the two bedrooms divided by a curtain. It was a poor neighbourhood, more crowded than the university campus I had been living on. One of the first things I saw was a freshly dead cat spewed across the busy road out front. It was not long before the corpse was flattened by cars and dried by the sun. I began looking for it each day as it became less and less recognizable. Finally, I could not tell the difference between the cat and an old bunch of dry leaves. Dust to dust. Ashes to asphalt.

They asked me at the hospital what I would do with your little body. I did not think my parents would want to deal with an official burial plot and stone. I thought about cremation, until a nurse gave me an approximate price for both. The cheapest option, she said, would be the hospital incinerator. Annabel, I had no money. I had to borrow afterwards to come to Japan. For days after, I scanned the city's smoke stacks for a trace of you.

*

The summer was supposed to be a time for thinking up solutions, but nothing came about easily. When my pregnancy was undeniably evident, the restaurant manager fired me. He swore it was because I broke too many glasses, but that was only an excuse. People are uncomfortable accepting food from a pregnant woman. We evoke visions of bodily fluids and bloody placentas.

Amy's friend Willa, who is a midwife, told me of societies where mothers routinely eat placenta tissue and rarely suffer from postpartum depression. She fried her own baby's placenta with onions. "It was a good sized steak," she said. "I had an energy high for days." Amy and I were going to try it, but I could not take your placenta home, when I was leaving you behind.

My parents wanted me to give you up for adoption. I did think about it. But after a few weeks with Amy, things changed. My summer of thought became one of sentience. All my senses were more acute, as though you were straining to feel through my flesh. Trees in the space of a streetlight could hypnotize me, spaghetti with artichokes brought tears to my eyes. And Amy's voice!

After I was fired, and no one else would hire me, I attended every gig like a devoted groupie. The bar noise was unbearable, and just when I thought I could not stand a second more, she would step out, and the music was hardly loud enough. Her voice would weave out through the harsh smoke and conditioned air, curling around me like steam from hot pavement in a summer rainstorm. Whenever you heard her, you would still your poking limbs and listen, mesmerized.

Afterwards, we would catch the all-night bus, no odd couple among that late crew. Though I never saw anyone else who was pregnant. At home, Amy made sleepy tea to calm my prickly legs. If we turned out the lights, the raccoons would come, plod-plodding across the metal porch roof and climbing down the television antenna, buzzing their cicada-like chatter. Sometimes they would push their noses through the loose corner of the screen.

"They're not afraid," I whispered.

"No," Amy said. "Raccoons thrive in cities. No predators. They live longer than in the wild."

If we looked out, we could often see six or seven. The city was a dreamscape, ruled by a different race.

When you were jumpy, Amy would pull my shirt away from my stomach, which was lined like a striped watermelon, and spread out her callused guitar fingers. Then she would speak closely so that I felt her breath on my navel. Mostly she sang and told stories, till one night, she began making plans. "When you are born," she promised. "I'll give you a stuffed raccoon toy." Your whole watery world shuddered. For the first time, someone spoke as though you really would arrive.

After that, it was all plans. Where we were going to live, all the toys and books and music you would have. You two were co-conspirators. Only I held back. I could not quite see it, a room with a crib and white curtains. Yet I was aware of you at every moment, not just curled in my belly, but through my whole body. When I was four and my mother was pregnant with my brother, I remember thinking that his head must be up inside her breast where he could drink. It seemed to me you were everywhere, your fingertips reaching through mine. My skin became soft and perfect like yours.

Amy suggested a home birth. "Our new place will have to be sound-proof," Amy said. "Just imagine you in labour at four o'clock some morning, hollering until all the neighbours call 911!"

My laughter caught short in my throat. I considered the pain.

Willa listened to your heartbeat and felt the position of your head. "If you're worried about anything specific you should have an ultrasound."

I shook my head. I had not been to a doctor once, not even to confirm the pregnancy. I did not need to.

*

Should I buy you a Jizo figure and tend it the way the Japanese do? What do you need to be protected from now? I am not very enthusiastic about Buddhism, the abnegation of earthly desire, when most of all I desire to feel your swish inside my body again.

I prefer to climb the narrow steps that continue up the hills, higher than the Buddhist temples where monks and tourists bustle. Here I am nearly alone, with no other human company, at least. The Shinto shrines are smaller, deeper into the woods and hills. Carved faces are sharp and beaked, and figures are winged. Not like the smooth, passive Buddhas. Shinto is full of spirits and imaginary creatures. Mischievous water monsters are called kappa. They have been known to drown children, dragging them down to the river bottoms.

*

I dreamt that you were a toddler, but you looked at me with a grown-up face, a look of sympathy. I awoke with a pain in my lower back, and my first thought was that you were unusually still. I did not want to wake Amy, we had been out late the night before. But the pain was spreading to my abdomen, and my watermelon stripes were rippling. I pulled the curtain aside and called her softly. "Amy. Something's wrong."

As I stood, a smelly warm liquid began trickling down my leg. Amy dialed Willa's number and hung up quickly. "Willa said to call an ambulance."

The world tilted and rocked with surges of pain. I remember the next several hours only in glimpses, blacking in and blacking out of consciousness, while you left my body.

They x-rayed you, and a matter-of-fact doctor told me: "The diaphragm was the main problem. There was a large hole, and all of her abdominal organs were forming high up in the chest cavity. When the time came for her lungs to develop, there would have been no space. If she had gone to full term, she would have had no lungs."

Flesh from the dust, but no breath of God would ever fill you.

"I'm surprised you held on to her as long as you did," the doctor continued. "Usually a woman's body expels a fetus with such a serious problem much earlier in the pregnancy."

Then he let me see you. You were white with faint blue veins and transparent fuzz for hair. You looked like an opal with its inner light flickered out. Amy snuck in then. She had been waiting all day. She took me home, drawing stares on the subway for holding my hand. It began to pour as we left the station, but we didn't bother to run. Lightning raged, glowing green and eerie in the summer night. It looked like your soul flashing through the sky to wherever it is you are now.

It was nearly midnight. Amy made me change into a dry T-shirt and pulled me down to her futon. From behind she put her arms around my waist and her knees into the back of mine. We tried to sleep, but I could not. *Rachel is weeping for her children. She refuses to be comforted, because they are no more.* The rain continued and the raccoons did not look in.

*

I dream of Amy, the way I left her at the airport. She had just kissed me on the lips in front of all those people. I could not look back. It used to thrill me to step aside in a mall, and see someone I loved in a crowd, spot-lit by my feelings amongst the masses. It is different when you are about to put an ocean between you.

Amy moved her stuff to her sister's apartment. She and the band were going to go on tour. "If you ever get to Japan, I want a backstage pass," I said. Most of our words were feeble in that last week.

There is always some pathetic Japanese salaryman imitating Elvis with the karaoke microphone at the bar. Occasionally, a hostess will get up out of boredom, and I get nervous. Worried that even the slightest depth of passion in a good voice might remind me of Amy, and send me off in a flurry of tears. There is no need. None of these blonde Australians look or sound anything like her.

A few more months of this, and I will have enough money to leave. Pretty ears are worth a lot in this land of methodical self-dissolution. I do not want nirvana. I will re-gather myself and return. Amy will be waiting in the crowd at the airport with a stuffed raccoon in her arms.

I will have come full circle around the world, and in

time. To the right time. And you, Annabel, will return to the secret place beneath my heart and diaphragm to grow. You will return, my heart's desire.

BLACKBERRY WINE

I wake up at the far end of the first explosion and moments before the next. The sheets are soaked with blood, and my brain so hammers the inside of my skull that I do not know whether the blasts have occurred inside my body or out. I do not want to move, the sun angles through the blinds and my soggy eyelids like daggers. But I had better check on Gran.

She is not in her bed, nor is she in the kitchen. I do not see her in the front or back yards. That leaves the basement. I pull the frayed light cord which does little to cheer the steep concrete steps.

"Granny?" The fruit cellar door is shut, but there seem to be gurgles of activity behind. I try the handle. Locked. "Are you in there?" Just as I slouch against the door, a third blast hits from the inside and splits my head from ear to ear. I scrunch my eyes shut with the pain and sway, touching my hand to the wall for balance while a cramp rakes through my abdomen.

"Gran? Are you in there?" I breathe short quick breaths like a woman in labour, and pound the door with panic. Yet underneath I feel a current of calm, as if I know she cannot really be in there. I stop, and all I hear is a faint fizzling from the other side.

I had better call someone. My mother. But if I do that, she is sure to attract a hasty entourage of uncles and aunts, too many of whom live nearby. I cannot have them descending upon me in this state, sweating clammily, hair plastered to my forehead, and blood showing on my pajama leg even below my robe.

In the bathroom, I peel off the sticky pajamas and drop them in the tub. Then I strip the bloody sheets from my bed, and rinse them as well. What I really need is a shower, but that would take too long, and Gran might be in trouble after all. I splash my face and thighs with cool water, pull on a pair of shorts and a T-shirt, and return to the phone, to dial home. "Mom? Is Granny there?"

*

They decided Gran was senile when she stopped going to church. There had been other incidents. Uncle Frank would draw circles in the air beside his temple and say, "Mom's gone a bit wonky again." Like the time she flung every doily she owned out the nearest window, then circled the house, raking them into a garbage bag. They were slightly more miffed when she sold her wedding china at a garage sale. She said she had always hated it. But it was the Sunday morning when Tom found her turning over the garden in Grandpa's old overalls, instead of properly hatted and gloved in the pew, that sparked the meeting.

Gran would never agree to a professional caregiver, but my mother had a thrilling suggestion. "We could send Ann! Not to take care of her, just to keep a quiet eye." And report on any serious digressions, I thought. This was my reward for reaching puberty with relative obedience and good behaviour. I got to babysit a crazy old lady, full time, no less, and without pay. The only advantage I could think of was that I would not have to go to church.

Instead, on the first Sunday, Gran came into my room extra early, and shook me so that my teeth clacked against each other. "Up!" she said. "Blackberries are ripe. Might as well put you to work."

Obviously, she had not been fooled for a second. She resented her children's presumptions on her privacy and I would have to pay. "Why should I be punished?" I asked.

Gran laughed at me. "It's only a punishment if you decide to see it that way." I did see it that way, so I took a long time getting dressed. But I did not dare to disobey her altogether.

The blackberries dominate the empty lot behind Gran's house. Grandpa used to hack them back with a machete, but since his death the berries have encroached upon the yard. They are too thick to get very far among them, but lucky for me, so abundant that it takes days to clear the fruit just from the edges.

"This patch of blackberries is all the church I need!" Gran exclaimed once we were out in the hot sun filling margarine containers with the fruit.

I was furious. My fingers were already cut up and there were several stains on my shirt. "What about all these prickles?"

Gran laughed, loud and long. "We need those prickles, child, to keep us here. Otherwise we'd be off to heaven before our time."

She never used to be crazy, I thought. She used to sit quietly and knit us all socks.

*

"When is the last time you saw her?" My mother shrills over my shoulder, rushing me down the basement steps. Uncles Tom and Frank are already ahead of us, Aunts Tina and Martha behind.

"Last night. Late. About two this morning, really," I admit. My mother's look opens with incredulity and turns quickly to disapproval. But she says nothing, because we have reached the fruit cellar. The uncles take turns pummeling the door with their shoulders until the hinges whine and the door falls. Fat Frank sprawls on top like a dropped caterpillar. At the sight inside, Tina starts howling and everyone clamours for a view. The ceiling and walls are streaked with purple-red gore and fruit from shattered bottles of preserves. "The wine!" I gasp.

All that work blown to smithereens. When we had picked all the berries we could reach, Gran took them to the basement and put them through a small blender. She then poured the mush through cheese cloth into three large buckets. I had to stand upstairs at the stove, stirring pound after pound of sugar into boiling water until it showed floating white formations, too saturated to dissolve anymore. As if picking for several hours each day, scraping my arms to ribbons, and ruining all my summer clothes wasn't enough! It was a good thing Gran was downstairs, because I felt like holding her head in that pot until it dissolved. The air was like syrup. Sweat poured down my face to my mouth where sweet and salt mingled cloyingly. Sickening. I closed my eyes, but all I could see were blackberry bushes lining the insides of my eyelids like wallpaper.

I did not understand how Gran could justify doing all that work, making me do all that menial work, for something that wasn't even substantial. Something that made you crazy and drunk. Something that may have blown Gran to kingdom come. We hunt among the ruins, treacherous glass shards and mashed fruit. Gran is not there.

We trudge upstairs, trying to decide what to do. My

brother and father appear at the front door. "Why, in heaven's name, were you up till two?" my mother remembers to demand, and everyone starts exclaiming and complaining.

"We were siphoning the wine," I say. My voice has become hoarse.

"That blasted wine," Tom says and starts to chortle. "Get it? That blasted wine? Get it?" He elbows Tina next to him, and everyone glares. They all think Tom is showing signs of following in his mother's footsteps these days. "You know, they say there's a Model A buried in those blackberries. Neighbour parked it when he went overseas to fight. By the time he got back it had disappeared," Tom adds. They pointedly ignore him.

"Call the police," Martha says.

"Not yet." Frank holds up his hands as if to calm everyone. "We have to do some looking first. She may have just wandered off and got lost."

"Maybe she just forgot to tell Ann where she was going," my father says. "She didn't think she needed Ann here to begin with." I sink to a chair and put my head between my knees while the conversation swishes around.

"What's wrong with you?" My mother shakes me some time later. When I open my scratchy eyelids, the room is crowded with many more people than earlier. They are standing in clusters, discussing search plans. How can I announce that I am suffering from the combined havoc of my first splintering hangover and narrow-hipped menstrual hell?

"Cramps," I whisper, thinking I can confide in my own mother.

"Darryl!" Mom calls across the room, loudly so that everyone stops talking and looks. "Pop home, will you?

And get your sister the Pamprin?" I put my red head back between my knees.

The searchers organize. Tina sits with the phone and Gran's address book. Martha heads upstairs, just to take one more look around the house. I pray she doesn't find the stained, wet sheets. They might think I killed Gran. I follow the crowd outside just in case. Frank divides people up and sends them in different directions, with special concentration on the wooded gully down the block.

Darryl returns on his bike and tosses a plastic bottle at my head. "Here, Ragweed!" I glare, but I'm grateful. I return to the kitchen, where I swallow two pills for my cramps, and two more for my hangover.

Minutes later, a local television news team arrives, rapid-firing questions I can't keep up with. When they head out to the gully for some ominous pictures, I stay behind and float up the stairs. As my headache recedes, I try to work through what happened last night.

*

The wine tasted sweet and sharp, of berries and thorns. "That's last year's batch," Gran told me, topping my glass to the brim once again. "No two batches are the same."

After adding the sugar and yeast, the fruit had to sit and ferment for over a week. I finally found some respite from Gran's hectic work routine. When Gran siphoned the wine from the buckets, all I had to do was move the clean tanks into place. And sip. I savoured the unfamiliar warmth of alcohol at the back of my throat.

When she finished filling the tanks, Gran screwed on plastic lids to keep out contaminants, and gave a huge sigh. She sat down in that unladylike way she had of late, knees wide apart, and poured herself a glass of wine. “For the redemption of our sins,” Gran said, holding the bottle as high as she could above the glass without spilling. I was mesmerized. “Is this your first communion?” Gran cackled, and took a big gulp.

I laughed involuntarily at the blasphemy. Lightning could have struck the house. Maybe that was why we were hiding in the basement. Gran emptied her glass and looked around at all her glowing jewelly jars, reflecting a rainbow on her face. “We should smash our glasses against the hearth, like the Italians, I think it's the Italians,” Gran said, but she refilled them instead.

I pictured the Lord's Supper at my parents' church ending with a great joyous crash of tiny glasses hurled at the pulpit. Instead, everyone always tried so hard to mute the mere clicking of glass on wood when they slipped the cups into the holders on the back of each pew. This sweet razzle of blackberries was nothing like the vinegary smell of the church wine.

“Who am I?” Gran asked. She had bulged out her eyes and pulled her chin in to create an extra fold. I laughed and sputtered burny wine out my nose. The resemblance to Uncle Frank solemnly swallowing his teeny mouthful of wine and self-consciously covering a burp was amazing. “Or how about this one?” Gran wrinkled her forehead into a crease of concern and pursed her lips. I was staring at my mother. “I used to look just like her,” Gran said. She winked and lifted the bottle for another refill.

I don't remember much more about the night besides laughing and drinking too much. I know Gran walked behind me up the stairs with her arms out to catch me in case I fell. She also undid my shorts in the bathroom so that I would not pee my pants. When she left me in my bedroom, she said she was returning to the fruit cellar to replace the temporary screw lids with fermentation valves, otherwise the three tanks of wine would explode. She knew those valves were in the kitchen somewhere. Gran must not have made it down to the fruit cellar. That was at two a.m.

*

The pain has faded and my brain feels cushiony, my eyelids like satin pillowcases, rippling smoothly. The wallpaper buzzes with flower chains and borders. When I slept in this room as a child, on special occasions, I found that I could squint at the wall so that it buckled into a third dimension and a secret hallway appeared. As soon as I blinked, the wall would flatten again. I thought I had lost this ability, but now, with my head spinning on a feathery cloud, the wall opens. It is remarkably easy and the vision stays, even when I close my eyes. I stand and enter the winding, narrowing corridor. Soon the vines and flowers of the print poke out of the walls, stringing right across so that I have to duck and push them aside to get by. Finally, I am trapped, live wallpaper strapping me in on all sides. But I remember peacefully that I am dreaming and shake myself awake.

I am very warm. My face feels shiny and my limbs like lead. My back window overlooks the backyard and the berries which spread over several lots. Far out, in the middle flutters a piece of light-coloured cloth, rosy with twilight.

*

It takes a backhoe. Several of the searchers try to wade in, but the sharp thorns quickly turn them away. Frank finds his father's rusty machete and hacks away, succeeding only in sticking himself a few feet in. The television crew returns for live coverage when a neighbour drives the beast around the house, cutting deep, muddy tracks in the lawn. He digs far enough in to set Gran free. She sits in the scoop for the ride back.

Gran looks tiny and tired under Tom's protective arm, but she insists she does not need a hospital. The drops of blood along her arms and legs are thorn scratches, superficial. She goes to bed, warm and fed, and finally everyone leaves her to rest. I wait while the family gathers in the living room, eyeing me suspiciously. I wonder how I will convince them to let me stay.

SINGLES' CLUB

Two days before her thirty-fifth birthday, Lois decides she must end her state of virginity. Not in small, nosy Dunnville, but somewhere large and impersonal. New York City would be the most logical choice, but that might spoil it for her, and she has always wanted to go there. She pulls out a stack of unused road maps. Southern Ontario, upstate New York. It has to be somewhere she would never want to go to again, she thinks. Buffalo.

Yesterday, Lois arrived at work early so she could find a new cassette for her answering machine. She murmured good-morning to Karla, the cashier. Girls like Karla intimidate her: fashionable, made-up, confident. Lois does not know where they find that source of boldness. She is too self-conscious for dramatic clothes or colourful makeup, and unrehearsed exchanges with strangers.

"Wow! Another tape?" Karla exclaimed, ringing the purchase in with hands arched to accommodate the nails. "Maybe you should get the other brand. That's what I've got, and I've reused it hundreds of times."

"I don't reuse them," Lois admitted.

"What?"

Lois felt the blood creeping up against her skin. "I save them so that I can keep track of all the messages. I don't want to forget anyone."

Karla's jaw dropped and Lois could see her fillings. Likely from chewing all that gum, Lois thought. "You save all of them?" Karla said. "Wow! Where do you keep them? My whole house would be full!"

Lois shrugged and rushed to her narrow, fluorescent lit office behind the pharmacy counter, her refuge. She felt stupid for exposing herself. Karla would think she was a moron. Lois imagines the high school girls who work in the drug store must pity her. Over thirty, no boyfriend or prospects, awkward and undeniably silly. God, I wouldn't want to end up like that, she hears them saying. Karla would surely spread this latest strange story.

Actually, Lois had only one small shoebox full of tapes. Most of the messages came from the town's automated library system, disjointed voices saying her books are overdue. The others were from her mother, or Margaret who would complain to anyone, even a lifeless box. She knew it was ridiculous to save them, but the disappointment of coming home to that unblinking red light was sometimes overwhelming. Although she had never yet pulled out an old one to soothe her loneliness, she expected that one day she would.

At noon, two teenaged boys rang the bell at the pharmacy counter. Lois approached them warily. She usually felt safe in her invisibility to young boys, but these wanted to ask her a question. "We need you to help us settle a bet," said the one with the leather jacket. "We saw this movie where this girl overdoses on heroin. This guy she's with gets this giant needle of something and sticks it in her heart to revive her, and it works. She jumps across the room."

"He says it's fake," said the blonde one, "that it's just a movie thing, but I think they can really do things like that."

"You know all about drugs, don't you?" Leather Jacket asked.

Lois responded nervously. "A shot of adrenaline directly into a muscle can revive a person if their breathing and heart-rate are depressed. I've never heard of plunging it into a person's heart."

"But it's possible, right?" the blonde one said excitedly.

"I don't really know," Lois said. Neither boy was satisfied, and they continued arguing as they left. Lois wished she had just said *yes*. The only time she had witnessed a life-saving application of adrenaline there were no dramatic heart plunges or slim movie stars. Only Miss Hulde, the high school typing teacher, object of scorn. She always wore white blouses with collars that tied into great floppy bows in front. She was sitting in church in one such blouse in the middle of the Lord's Supper, when she suffered an anaphylactic reaction. Doctors later determined that the chunks of bread must have come in contact with nuts in the bakery. She shook, splashing her tiny cup of wine on her white blouse. A nearby nurse took a kit from Miss Hulde's purse, then pulled up her skirt and jabbed a needle into her thigh. Sprawled on the pew, with her skirt up and bloodied with wine, she was in view of the whole church. Though her life was saved, the congregation squirmed, and her students never forgot those exposed thighs.

There were no messages when Lois arrived home, but her disappointment was stemmed by the fact that it was Thursday. Her church's Singles' Club met Thursdays. Lois no longer expected to find romance at the club. There was always the chance that someone new and dashing would show up, but most members had known each other and their failings far too long to pair up and date. Instead as a group, they focused their frustration in love on other endeavours. Charities, bible study, singing. Lois especially liked to take her guitar and tap into that stream of passion which precluded sex and social acceptance. For a while.

She had just put a porkchop in the microwave when the phone rang. It was her mother. "Lois, who is this Dirk Verhoef?"

"What?"

"Dirk Verhoef, he says he knows you."

"Oh," Lois called a face to mind. "He goes to the church. He just started coming to Singles lately."

"He is a special friend of yours?"

Mr. Verhoef was a fussy, arrogant man, and was older than anyone else in the group. He peered through eye-bulging glasses from a beard and mustache that seemed to cover his entire face. Many were surprised when he started showing up at the club meetings. Lois grimaced at the thought of him. "No, not really," she said.

"That's very odd," her mother hesitated. "He called here last night and asked to speak to your father, all very formal. He asked permission to marry you."

Lois felt deep rumblings of shame in her stomach. "You're joking, right?"

"No," her mother, who was holding back, started to chuckle.

"He must be fifty years old! He's . . . he's . . ." Lois sputtered for the word, but could only find one she had not used in twenty years. "He's gross!" She could hear her mother conveying this information to her father, and the ensuing laughter. "What did you say to him?" she asked.

"Your father said you make most of your own decisions these days. I guess he'll be asking you soon!" her mother laughed. "Let us know if you accept."

Lois groaned and hung up. Her evening was ruined. In fact, in retrospect, so were the past few weeks' meetings, although she had enjoyed them at the time. The sleigh-ride at a local farm had seemed so exhilarating. She had led the Singles in singing, and everyone looked rejuvenated and no one, not even Margaret, was cranky. Now all she could remember was how Mr. Verhoef (he had never asked them to call him Dirk) kept propping up cushions for her and even set the beat with his foot for each song before she could begin. Creepy. He had been watching her.

She cannot possibly go, she thought, he might try and make a move. But somewhere a tiny spot of anger changed her mind. In Dunnville, she would surely encounter him sooner or later. She would go and get it over with. She left for the meeting without her guitar, deciding she would feign a sore throat. The small dim room in the church basement with the crickety steam radiator and the smell of coffee, both old and perking, had always been cozy in the past. This time, it was ugly, drafty and claustrophobic. Lois could feel Mr. Verhoef's buggy gaze on her, and her mad courage started to waver. At the end of the meeting, she turned down donuts and tried to escape. Mr. Verhoef hurried after. She felt a wave of fear on hearing his footsteps coming up the church basement stairs behind her.

"Lois," he called, and caught up. "I'll walk you home."

A statement, not a question, Lois thought. She smiled politely at him anyway. She did not know what to say to him, and it hardly mattered, once he started talking.

"I've really enjoyed attending these meetings. I've especially enjoyed your singing and guitar playing. I'm very sorry you didn't play tonight." He looked at her questioningly.

"My throat . . ." Lois gestured towards her neck.

Mr. Verhoef shrugged. "For years I could have come

to these meetings, but I was concentrating on my business. I'm a plumber, you know."

Lois nodded.

"I've been doing well lately, and I've started to think about other things. That's why I decided to come." He paused, but only briefly. "Of all the women in the club, you are the one who impresses me most."

No beating around the bush, Lois thought. She shivered and buried her face into her jacket collar, though the air had a hint of the mulchy warmth of earliest spring. She looked up only to see how much longer he had to talk. They were halfway to her apartment.

"There's the singing of course, but you are also a very pleasant and reasonable girl. That's why I think you would be good for me. You know, I can't really expect to get one of those teenagers, at my age." He chuckled. "What do you say?"

Lois stared at the ground, away from his hairy presence. She felt outraged, but expressions of anger never crossed her lips, and they did not know how to now. "I really don't think we are right for each other," she said quietly.

"Don't you want to get married?" he demanded.

"No."

He huffed. "Well, I believe your house isn't much further. I think I'll go see if Margaret needs an escort." He walked away.

Lois ran home and pushed her door tightly behind her. She could not understand why she felt so completely humiliated.

*

In the morning, she called in sick, and it was not entirely a lie. She felt nauseous and achy, and could only pull herself out of bed to draw a bath. She closed her eyes and let herself feel the water lapping against all her unexplored crevices. She was not overweight, her features were neat and regular. Just a bunch of plain parts amounting to an unspectacular sum. Yet in thirty-five years, the only proposition of any kind from a man was an ugly, disgusting joke. Which part of her was to blame?

She did not quite know where the last decade had gone. At university, she was devoted to her textbooks and too shy to meet people. When she returned, thinking herself successful for having snagged a professional job in the area, everyone else from high school had paired up, and formed symmetric groups drinking coffee after church. Lois wondered if they spoke of her the way they used to deride their old maid teachers. "All she needs is a good roll in the hay!" they used to say.

Her failure was never one of imagination. Even while studying for exams, she allowed herself short breaks to conjure an intriguing face, from somewhere far from Dunnville. England maybe. An intellectual or an artist who had fled some terrible heartbreak for the furthest thing he could imagine, a dairy farm in Southern Ontario. Lois enjoyed the details until she had to start drawing the dream into her reality. It never worked. There was never a foreign face in the congregation, though she scanned it every Sunday. In her world, women married ordinary men with similar backgrounds and families, and they never moved far.

She would have to change her reality.

*

Lois maps a careful route to Buffalo, using her finger first. She refuses to procrastinate, which would make her nervous, and leaves on Saturday afternoon. It is cold, but dry when she starts the car, though she would brave a blizzard just to get this over with. The scene is dreary once she leaves the town. Fields covered with thin snow, gray tufts of old grass poking through.

When she was little, she had fantasies about disguising herself to run away. She did not want to leave, she just liked to imagine all the details. How she would wear her brother's weak reading glasses and old clothes no one remembered. Their description to the police would be so far off, that no one would look twice at her. She could be the most successful runaway, if she wanted to. Now, she sparks so little interest that she does not need a disguise. She might as well be invisible climbing into her little car and leaving town.

In a week it will be spring. You would not know from the snowy surfaces, but Lois can sense something coming below. Some movement like the churning in her stomach. Her voice cracks at the border. She is sure the customs officer knows exactly what she is up to, but he waves her along, hardly looking. She took care to avoid coffee all morning, but it does not help. Instead of driving speedily along, she keeps stopping to pee. By the time she reaches Buffalo, there are half a dozen donuts on the seat beside her, each from a different shop. At one point, she is so desperate that she stops by the side of the road and crouches in a ditch, yellowing the snow like a dog. She has not seen another car for miles, but one appears out of nowhere and honks wildly, while Lois struggles with a wad of Kleenex.

She does not know Buffalo at all. She drives randomly, stopping briefly at a drug store for cosmetics, and condoms, stuff she could never buy at the store where she works. Back in her car, she begins looking for a hotel with a choice of restaurants and bars nearby. Everything seems dirtier, seedier than she had hoped. Finally she gives up and turns in at the next hotel she sees. It is not even three o'clock. She has hours to prepare.

In all her runaway fantasies, she never thought about a destination. She never imagined the hideous curtains of a cheap hotel room, or the clammy feel of the cool polyester bedspread. It does not take a minute to explore the room. No hidden treasures, just a bible in a drawer. She wants to rest after the nerve-wracking drive.

Lying flat on her back, she tries to manufacture a dream, this time uncensored. There will be no more limits on her reality. Before she sleeps, she conjures a picture of what tonight might be like. Sensuous, if not romantic. A clean and casual bar, lights low. Maybe some short candles in those tiny glass bowls. She cannot imagine his face, but she can think about what it will feel like when he touches her. She must not get excited too quickly and give herself away. The events, the movements take over. She sees his body, the weight of his arms against her, the hardness of his chest, his rough chin and lips, his . . . Mr. Verhoef. She jumps upright. She must have fallen asleep and let her fearful unconscious take over. A nightmare. Whatever else happens, she thinks, after tonight she will be rid of Mr. Verhoef for good.

She goes out for a sandwich, then returns to begin the preparations. Like Cleopatra oiling and perfuming her body, though the hotel room is hardly a royal bath. She blushes with shame each time she catches her eye in the mirror, before reminding herself that this must be done.

She tries on the eyeliner she bought at the drug store. She never wore it before because she once heard her mother say it made girls look like raccoons. The effect is startling. Her usually blurry face looks defined and polished. She decided carefully last night what she would wear. Good jeans and a simple blouse. No making a greater fool of herself by dressing in something fancy. Her undergarments give her the most doubt. Plain, white, sensible.

When she is finally ready, it is eight-thirty, and she heads out. She walks slowly past the bars. At the end of the block, she realizes she must simply choose one. *Hal's* is nearly empty, so she heads for a table in a corner. When a waitress approaches, she forgets what she has rehearsed and orders a coffee.

"To start," she adds apologetically, but the waitress does not seem to care. Lois pulls a magazine out of her purse. She is too early.

In anticipation of Easter, the news magazine has several articles about Christ controversies. Such talk has never been tolerated in the Calvinist church Lois is used to, where the accepted version of the bible is the literal word of God. There are no gory depictions of Christ in Calvin's world to spur debate over the nature of his body, but the article has photographs of artists' depictions. Caravaggio's *Doubting Thomas* pokes his finger into a grotesquely stretchy slot in Christ's side. This picture reminds her of her mission, and she glances around.

There are several men at the bar, all with their backs to Lois. It has to be now, before she loses her nerve she thinks, and gets up. She climbs onto a stool with her heart pounding and asks the bartender for a Corona, reading the name from a cardboard coaster. With magazine in hand, just in case, she looks around. Sliding over several faces, none of them mean anything to her. Maybe she thought there would be a sign on his forehead. She turns back to her magazine. Luckily, she has finished the Easter article and is on to the entertainment page when a man sits down beside her.

"What's so interesting about that magazine?" he asks, and arrogantly slides it out of her grasp. "Oh, movies! You seen that *Pulp Fiction*? Weird flick, man."

She clears her throat. "No, not yet."

"Well, you should," he looks at her face and he smiles. "I'm Ed."

"I'm Lois," she says, then remembers she was not going to use her real name.

Ed is wearing a plaid shirt, jeans, and tan coloured suede boots which he keeps lifting up against the bar and her stool, to show off. He buys her a beer, though she has barely touched her first, and continues to talk. The process is remarkably boring. He keeps urging her to drink more, though she is already feeling drowsy and constantly has to pee. Her back is sore from the backless stool.

At midnight, Ed reaches over and runs his finger down her arm. "So, Lois," he drawls, "what are you doing tonight?"

She giggles, foolishly. "I'm sitting here with you," she says.

"What would you think about a nightcap at my apartment? Just five minutes from here." Good, she thinks. I will be able to walk back to the hotel.

His apartment is above one of the restaurants she surveyed earlier, one room with an alcove for a kitchen. He takes two cans of beer from the low fridge and opens them. No glasses. After three hours of meaningless chat in the bar, she is wondering how much more will be required, when he begins pulling off his boots. He places them carefully beside the bathroom door. Then, to her amazement, he proceeds to undress. In a moment, he is naked. He takes her hand, pulling her up from the couch, which he then unfolds into a bed. He pats the space beside him for her to lie, then grins with droopy eyelids as he begins to undo her blouse. She thinks with panic of the condoms in her purse by the door, but he reaches over to a side table drawer and pulls out a condom of his own. This isn't so bad, she thinks.

Then he kisses her, but his mouth is not sexy at all, it is hard and bruising. He pulls off her bra and presses his hands over her breasts. She thinks, this can't be right. Right or wrong, he is too heavy on top of her to be pushed off. He pulls off her jeans and underpants together, scratching her hips with their roughness. He pauses only to snap on the condom, then he thrusts into her and smiles at her grunt. The pain is more than she could have imagined, and the only word in her mind is *brute*.

Just when she thinks she can no longer stand to be conscious, he finishes. Without opening his eyes, he flings the condom onto the floor, turns off the light and drops to sleep beside her.

She waits. Her vagina is burning, and she is painfully aware of all the crusty bits in his bed. When there is no doubt he has passed out, she climbs off the bed and gropes around for her clothes, gingerly to avoid the condom. Agonizing over each slight noise, she finds the tiny bathroom and flicks on the light so she can dress. Its beam does not reach the bed, but she can see the trail. Beside the door is a tan suede boot with a deep crimson drop of her blood on its toe. A tiny prick of revenge.

It is a short walk to her hotel. Drunken men are leaving the bars, and sticking in corners of the street. She ignores their calls and walks carefully, with stiff hips, trying to minimize chaffing of denim against her raw areas. Her hotel room is attractive after Ed's scummy apartment. She draws a hot bath and endures the stinging to climb in. A wisp of blood floats up from between her legs.

She sleeps late the next morning, her birthday, and the first Sunday in years she is not in church. Before crossing the border to home, she buys a New York City newspaper to look for things to do on her next weekend trip. When she reaches her apartment, the light on her answering machine is flashing. Her stomach flops. Could Ed have tracked her down?

It is Margaret, asking Lois to be her bridesmaid. She is going to marry Mr. Verhoef. Lois laughs and rewinds the tape to record over.

FAMILY COMPACT

When I sit by the open window, the traffic drowns them out. There are six of my aunts in the room, along with my mother who is hosting this year. Some aunts complain the busy street makes it dangerous for their children. Some aunts always complain. Now, shadowed against the sunny back window, their mouths produce only the hum of hot tires on asphalt.

"Chris, why don't you go out back with the others?" my mother says. I cannot actually hear her, but I know that is what she is saying. I do not want to go outside with the cousins. I would have to take part in the conversation.

All summer I have been stuck in gluey heat, wanting to move. In June, I stood on the edge of the driveway while Thomas VanHolt resurfaced the pavement. He took off his soaked T-shirt and warned me to stay back. I can still feel the stench and steam clogging my nostrils, like the black globs of tar which have stuck to my sneakers all summer. Tonight the house is thick with the smell of the pickles I helped Mom can this morning. School starts on Tuesday. I just want a chance to catch my breath. Brenda is in the driveway. We are planning to set up a tent once the guests are gone.

"Hi," Brenda says. "You smell like pickles."

I hold up my green hands. I thought they would get back to normal once I finished in the greenhouse for the summer. Dirt permanently ground in, nails perpetually broken, fingers full of cuts. Now you cannot see the dirt for the stain left by the brine. The vinegar stung my slicey thumbs, and the stink will stay for days.

There is a commotion when my dad's van pulls up and all seven men pile out. Cousins and aunts run to the front for kisses.

"Do they really drive all the way from Algonquin Park so cramped?" Brenda asks.

"So they say." Last week my dad made a show of pulling out his back pack. My brothers got a thrill out of playing with the zippers and pockets. I used to too. I saw my mother take his passport from a cabinet and put it beside his wallet.

"I thought you only needed passports to cross borders," I said. "Algonquin Park isn't even out of the province."

"It's always good to have ID with you," she said.

My mother does not even have a passport. She never goes anywhere.

I turn and meet my mother's gaze as she motions me over. She is not happy to see Brenda at this otherwise family gathering. Brenda does not know that I invited her without parental approval. "I want you to help with the corn," Mom says.

"But I have to keep Brenda company."

"There are plenty of people for company," she says. She gives me a little push inside. The kitchen is even hotter, full of steam from the pots of boiling cobs. I am worried about Brenda because the cousins do not like her. She is not Dutch and does not go to the Christian school. And her father is on city council. I begged my parents to let me switch over to the public high school with Brenda, but it was out of the question. I hate that tiny school where every last name is Dutch and nearly everybody is related. Those who are not marry each other after graduation.

"Isn't anyone else going to help?" I know I am whining as I lift a huge bowl of corn to take out back to the picnic table.

"Just go!" my mother says. I had better watch myself. After all, she has not actually said anything about Brenda's presence.

Later Brenda and I find a place at the very back of the yard, taking plates piled with food. We do not notice when my father quiets everybody down for grace and giggle when we realize the prayer is well underway. An aunt whips a piece of potato salad which hits me in the shoulder. This only makes us laugh more. I am tempted to whip it back.

"How long will they stay?" Brenda asks. The gathering at the other end of the yard is getting noisier as more beer appears. Babies begin crying, and my older cousins pull out guitars.

"Pretty late. Do you know how to put a tent up in the dark?"

"We might have to sleep under the stars," Brenda says.

"If only we could call up a thunderstorm to disperse them," I say.

"But then we'd have to camp in the rain," Brenda warns. I wouldn't mind.

We listen from far outside the circle of chattering and random strums. Somewhere a guitar or voice begins a thin melody that weaves and wavers, catching more as it moves around the circle, until they are actually singing. "Seek ye first the kingdom of God . . ." We talk about the constellations.

When the relatives finally leave, we go inside for the tent.

"You're setting it up now? It's pitch black!" My mother is irritated

Dad and a handful of uncles are still there, though all the aunts and cousins have left. Brenda is confused.

"They always stick around to gloat," I say.

"What do you mean?" Brenda asks.

I shrug. Two more men join the group. Not my relatives, although one is my boss, Mr. Langbrook. The other is Thomas of the sweaty shirt. I whisper to Brenda that Thomas makes deliveries for my boss. I have often watched him loading a van while skulking among the flowers I am supposed to be cutting. Once I was working in the office because Mrs. Langbrook had broken her arm, when Thomas stepped inside. He said nothing to me, but smiled so that I could hardly concentrate on the addresses I was typing. Restaurants mostly. Invoices reading: two dozen roses, three mixed bouquets. The notebook was different: two cases Scotch, one vodka. Mrs. Langbrook snatched that notebook away, saying, "That's not the right one." I do not tell Brenda this part.

"Where's your brother?" my boss is asking.

"Driving Mother home," my father says.

"Ah yes. Must take care of the Godmother!" Mr. Langbrook says and they all laugh. I grab the tent from its shelf and push Brenda towards the back door.

We finish the tent quickly despite the darkness. Zipping only the screen, we lie with our heads by the door so we can watch the sky outside.

"I wish the orchard was still there," Brenda says. The lot behind the yard is part of a huge property facing the next street over. It used to hold an old farm house and a peach orchard behind, with trees coming right up to the hedge. Our church bought the property and plowed everything over to build a new, larger church. The square blue building is almost complete. Letters spelling "Word of Life" were recently hoisted over the door.

"Are you sleepy?" I ask.

"I don't want to be."

"Me neither. This is my last chance of freedom for another year. I want to do something exciting."

Brenda giggles. "I could dare you to do something."

"You can't come up with anything exciting enough," I say. I have carried out several of Brenda's dares through the summers. The most daring was walking the circumference of the yard completely naked.

"We could leave the yard," Brenda suggests.

"And go where?"

"Where the orchard used to be."

"There's nothing left there to hide behind," I warn.

"We'll just have to conjure up the spirits of the trees for cover," Brenda says with that spooky tone that makes me shiver.

"Okay. We get to at least carry our clothes with us." Chicken. But it would not be fun if we really got caught. Brenda seems to agree. We both take our shorts and T-shirts off and roll them up to carry. Looking at each other, we hesitate, then remove our underwear and bras which we leave inside the tent. The air is warm and humid, but touching every spot and crevice, it makes my skin tremble. We have to put our sneakers on for the construction site. Brenda flicks on the flashlight.

"Don't turn that on unless we absolutely have to," I say. "It might attract someone." We reach the hedge which borders the plowed-over orchard.

"Oh, no," Brenda says when we reach the opening in the bushes. We are used to squeezing through only fully clothed. Stifling squeals, Brenda pushes through first and I follow.

"Well! I'm scratched in places I've never even seen before," I say.

Before us is the field of dirt and some tree stumps. There are piles of construction materials everywhere and several vehicles near the building. The excitement of exposure makes me giggle. The dirty field is a wasteland, barren and ugly in contrast to the rich navy of the star-speckled sky. I feel a desolation in looking. In earlier years we snuck out to play among the grass and trees. I know how a peach blossom looks against the moon.

We reach a stump and stop. At this point between summer and the confines of school, I am aware of how time is passing. I want to make something of this moment. Memorialize the thrilling sadness of being naked in the moonlight, with disaster all around. We need a ceremony.

Brenda says. "I wish we could build a fire."

I place the flashlight on the stump and flick it on. The beam shoots up to meet the moon, eventually.

"Now draw a circle," Brenda says. She grabs my hands across the stump and we walk to make a circle with our feet. Long and naked, I feel eerily graceful but for my large and clunky sneakers. Brenda stops and faces south. "Hail guardians of the South, Powers of Fire! We invoke you and call you!" she begins, and continues with an invocation for all four directions.

I am fascinated. Brenda knows so much that is interesting and beautiful. What if there really are tree spirits?

Brenda finishes her verses, then crouches by the stump, pulling me down with her.

"Do you sense something?" she asks.

I breathe deeply. "This prickly feeling." But neighbourhood noises are drawing us back. I reach out and flick off the flashlight. "I want to put my clothes back on," I say. Brenda is quick to agree, and we dress.

We walk toward the church, avoiding scattered boards and bricks. The dark block looms monstrously against the darker blue of the sky. Instinctively, we walk closer together.

"It doesn't look much like a church," Brenda says.

"More like a mall. They've got a gymnasium and a banquet hall so they can have all their weddings in there." Self-contained world. All-encompassing. I have three years of high school left before I will leave this city for university. Other girls will marry boys like Thomas in this mall. Yet sometimes I dream about Thomas's sweaty chest.

"Have you been inside?" Brenda asks.

"No. I dare you to walk down the aisle naked."

We find a window open on one side, and by standing on a metal can, we climb inside to the church's kitchen. With the flashlight we find our way to the sanctuary. Pews and pulpit are discernible in the pale street and moonlight shining though the tall windows.

"Here's your chance," Brenda says. She pulls off her T-shirt and struts down the aisle, twirling it at the imaginary congregation. I feel a hint of that queasiness I experience when church invades any thought about sex, that stab of guilt each time my body changes. I fight it by running up to the pulpit and pulling off my shirt. My breasts are just above the edge of the lectern. I press them against the cool wood and sing a hymn.

"Shhh!" Brenda is running up towards me. "It echoes in here. Someone walking past might hear us."

"They'll think it's a ghost," I say. "The soul of the virgin they've sacrificed in the foundations."

We leave the sanctuary and start exploring, through various rooms and down some stairs to the basement. Most parts are empty, but in one dark storeroom we find boxes. Stacks and stacks of them. Brenda reaches in the top of one and pulls out a bottle. She shines the flashlight on the label. Jack Daniels. “There are tonnes of them!” she says.

I had not suspected the church, though now it seems obvious. “Let’s take one back to the tent.”

A spasm of panic races through my neck when we hear voices and steps on the stairs. We crouch behind a box and barely have time to pull our T-shirts on before the voices are in the same room. Four men are moving more boxes. I recognize two of the uncles.

We try to remain still, but my calf cramps and I tilt, bumping the bottle in Brenda’s hand. Rough shuffling reveals our hiding place. The third man is my boss. He hardly looks at me.

“Who’s this?” he asks, grabbing Brenda’s arm and pulling her to her feet. She flinches at his touch and the bottle slips from her grip, smashing against the floor. Sticky liquor runs over my hand and against my shorts so that I am compelled to stand. That is when I see Thomas by the door. I am suddenly aware that I have no bra under my T-shirt.

I hear an uncle say Brenda’s father’s name.

“The councilor,” Mr. Langbrook says.

I look at Brenda who is shivering with fear. I want to reassure her, but how can I explain? It is amusing to watch them figure out what to do. I am nervous only when it occurs to me that my father might show up.

One uncle holds up his hand to take charge. “Pretty dangerous walking around a construction site at night.

Plenty of things to cut yourself on or trip over. Dirty nails to step on," he hesitates. "Your parents wouldn't be too pleased to hear about it." He looks directly at Brenda. "What would your parents do if they found out?"

Brenda shrugs nervously and says, "Probably ground me." All of the men are watching her closely.

"You'd be grounded for a long time," the uncle continues, and stops again to gather his words. "Guess we scared you pretty badly catching you here," he says and waits for Brenda to nod. "Maybe we can make a deal. You wouldn't want to start the school year grounded. Tell you what, we won't tell your parents if you go and promise never to sneak around here again."

His patronizing tone makes me sneer. Brenda looks confused, but she will not turn down the offer. Maybe I will explain to her later that she need not worry. No one will ever tell her parents.

The uncle turns to me, smiling with his authority.

"Chris, the same goes for you. I know your father would be awfully mad to find you here. What do you say?"

"Throw in a bottle of whiskey and no one will speak another word," I say.

Shock flickers across everybody's face, and for a few moments, no one says a word. The men stare at me, newly appraising. I know I have them. I have never felt more powerful.

This uncle is quick. He laughs as he reaches for a bottle. "Might as well have fun while the summer's still on." He hands me the whiskey and shakes my sticky green hand. Brenda looks like she will faint with amazement. I wonder whether Thomas is impressed.

"Which way is out?" I ask.

Without a word, the other uncle opens the door and leads us outside. I smile at Thomas as we pass. In the parking lot I glance back to see my father's van turning in.

"I can't believe it! What just happened?" Brenda says when we are out of earshot. "Chris?"

I will have to tell her. Right now, I do not want to think. I open the bottle and take a drink. Heat streaks from my throat through my chest and stays. I have decided that I will refuse to work in the greenhouse next summer.

LIFE CHAINS

Aria floats five inches above her bed, hovering between worlds. I am afraid she will float away completely, or awake in a bruising crash after sailing over the guard rail. Every night I feel the tugging from her dreams into mine, and I surface in a panic, fighting to hold her back or catch her safely. Before my eyes are open, I am half out of bed. I will not rest again without checking on her. She is fast asleep, her head solidly on her pillow and not above. But it is no wonder I am always dreaming that she will fade away. At three-and-a-half, Aria is fragile and thin with origami delicacy. Her skin is pale, her limbs translucent. I pull up the bedclothes she has kicked away, and add an extra heavy blanket to weigh her down.

My mind is charged with worries that feed my insomnia when I return to bed. It would be comforting if Eric would wake enough just to murmur a few words when I am alone in the dark, but he never does, no matter how frequently I toss back and forth. All Aria has to do to wake me is twitch a foot. When she has nightmares, I can smell them brewing and am at her bedside before her eyes fly open. But her cries seldom wake Eric. What if I ever have to leave her alone with him? She could be whimpering in the grip of some cold darkness, and left there alone while her father snores. She is too young to know how to escape a nightmare on her own. She could disappear into its black whirling hole forever. Eric rolls his eyes when I express my concern. "If there's actually a problem, she'll howl loud enough," he says. He does not consider a nightmare a problem.

It is this wretched trip Eric's been planning. Since he got that teaching job, he has got two summer months off, and grand plans for the holidays. Grand in scale, not in glamour. Backpacking in Mexico. He sprang it on me in spring when the tulips waved Aria's first unfettered sprint around the spongy lawn. Last year, she always held my hand. She rushed among the flowers and sank in feet deep, her pristine frilly ankle socks gleefully muddied.

"I figure we could go the second week in July," he said, dangerously preoccupied while clipping the hedge. "That way we'd have a couple weeks leeway if we wanted to stay more than a month."

"What about Aria?" I asked. I stood beside a lawn chair, leaping with Aria's every move, as though she held invisible strings to a marionette.

"What about her? It would be a great experience for her." Snip, snip, brutally pruning poor young buds.

"Toddlers don't need great experiences." I shuddered at the horrors clamouring for attention inside my head. Flipping buses, dysentery, armed guerrillas. They blocked out the warm spring sun. "It would be dangerous."

Eric rolled his eyes and clamped his lips. He has such contempt for my weaknesses. "It's not dangerous," he said, dripping condescension on my fears as though that would hold them down. "But if you want, we don't have to take her. We can leave her with your mother."

"For a month?" I asked incredulously. "Do you know how long a month is to a child? She would think we had abandoned her or died. If it was a week, maybe," I conceded.

Eric snorted, a little warning flex of his anger that shuts like a heavy steel fire door when something interferes with his plans. "I'm not going down there just to turn around and come back after a week. We wouldn't get to see anything. I thought you were the one who wanted to go to Mexico in the first place!" He went to the shed and tossed the clippers inside in disgust and a racket of wrenching metal.

He was right. Central America was my area of expertise, my major in university. There is still a poster on the wall above my desk of an ancient sculpture of the Aztec Coatlicue, dressed in writhing snakes and adorned with human sculls. Goddess of birth and of death. Before graduation, I wanted nothing more than to tour the crumbling sites of my fascination. "That was before Aria," I said.

"What are you going to do? Put your life on hold until she grows up? I'm not going to wait twenty years to live again!" he shouted and tramped back into the house, heedless of the mud. I spoke cheerily to Aria. Maybe she had not heard.

*

Now it is June, and Eric's plan has blossomed as though I never had any objections. In the morning he says he will be late coming home. "I've got an appointment with this travel agent who specializes in these backpacking things," he says.

I turn away without a word and lift Aria down from her booster seat. I am much too tired to argue, too weak to resist the steel door's weight. Eric leaves, and Aria takes herself down to the basement to play. I stand and stare at the front window, knowing the dim rooms will be blinded with spots when I turn back. As I watch, there is a screech and scramble of movement on the front porch. I reach the windowsill just in time to see a smudge of brown feathers go over the side of the front steps.

The neighbour's cat darts away when I open the door, and I find a bird lying on the concrete. Its eyes are stunned, its head tilts back awkwardly, and dark blood gushes from its beak. Its wings slowly lower to its sides. Instinctively, I stroke the bird's breast, to comfort its dying moments. When its shuddering stops, I realize it was a stupid thing to do, projecting the need for heavy human touch on the airborne creature. It was likely as terrified of me as of the cat. Tears catch my throat. I know it is a part of the natural cycle of things. Cats catch birds, they kill them, they eat them. I look around for the cat to see if maybe I can coax it back, as though the cat's return to devour the bird would make the death more acceptable. But the cat is gone, and the corpse has no role.

The sun is growing hot, and all I can think of are the bird's insides beginning to bake, the blood coagulating in its throat. I had better get rid of it before Aria decides to play outside. From the kitchen I take a dustpan, then listen for the child at the top of the stairs. I do not like to leave Aria out of hearing for even a few minutes. But she seems fine, prattling away to some friend of her imagination.

Funny, I did not mind touching the bird while it was alive, but now that it is limp and lifeless, I feel squeamish. I slide the dustpan awkwardly under its body, flipping it up like a pancake away from the edge. With a small garden spade from the garage, I begin to dig in the soil under the back hedge, but the ground is harder and stonier than I expected. When I place the bird in the shallow trough, there is not enough dirt alone to cover it. I have to include the rocks, and the resulting grave is a messy, kickable hump. I am too dizzy to fix it.

I lie back on the grass to still the harsh corners insomnia has etched inside my skull. I shield my spinning eyes from the sun. When I can see again, the hedge looming above reminds me of the trees which clustered along the far border of my childhood yard. My sister Elizabeth always went first through the prickle branches to the hidden clearing where Dad had constructed a sandbox. One afternoon, when I climbed through the low pines, I found a dainty blue egg. I was holding it in my palm, looking up for a nest when Elizabeth came bumbling back to see what had stopped me.

"What's that?" Elizabeth reached roughly and snatched the egg, dripping yoke over my hand. "Oh! I thought it was a marble."

While Elizabeth knelt to examine the delicate shards of shell, I looked up in agonized panic for the egg's mother. I was terrified by the thought of her anguished mourning. I did not see her then, nor in the weeks I continued to watch. But I could feel her, feel her pain bulging my veins. When I stand, I almost fall again, but the ebbing black-out is quickly dazzled away by the sun in the corners of my eyes. Stunning like the canary-yellow jumpsuit Elizabeth wore so often that last summer.

*

Eric is excited when he comes home. "This guy's been all over Central America. He had some great tips." He watches me. There is a glittered edge to his eyes that is waiting, challenging me to respond.

I bite my lip and refuse, narrowing my attention to the food on the stove. He gives in and settles on the couch with the newspaper, but the atmosphere is still charged with agitation. Even the insects in the room have picked up on the vibrations, buzzing loudly, erratically. "What is that?" Eric asks, voice laced with irritation.

"What?"

"That whining. Some kind of bug." He is rolling up the newspaper and leaning forward on his seat. With my lifesaving margarine container, I hurry around the corner. I have to find it first. While he tightens his weapon, I zero in on the corner of the windowsill, beside some books. The wasp is in the grips of a spider rapidly winding it with sticky thread. "Oh!" I wail. Like the wasp, I am trembling and paralyzed. If I set the wasp free, I'll be depriving the spider of its natural food source, interfering in the chain of life. But that frantic buzzing! I cannot decide what to do.

Eric decides for me. Coming up behind me, he snatches the container and scoops it around the wasp, tearing roughly through the spider's web. He opens the window and tosses the wasp out, still wrapped in sticky thread, its wings glued down and helpless. "What did you do that for?" I say. I can hear the hysteria in my voice.

"Because it was driving me nuts!" Eric yells. He whips the container towards the kitchen, then begins to unroll the paper he was reading.

*

After dinner, I haul Aria off to get ready for bed as soon as possible. I slump against the tub with exhaustion, oblivious to the great waves Aria sends over the side, soaking me in her exuberance. She is still going strong, heaving herself back and forth to rock the flotilla of plastic boats, tiny armless people falling overboard in droves. I rest my head on my arms and watch. Aria's blue vein-traced skin looks rosier than usual, almost ruddy in the cheeks. But this might be just the blurring film across my eyes. I feel so lifeless in comparison.

Aria's struggles in the bath towel sap all that I have left. Her hair is still wet and uncombed when I dump her on her bed with a pile of books, and head for my own bedroom. A throbbing ensues in the upper right corner of my brain, like a hard boiling egg in my skull. As soon as I close my eyes the egg becomes Elizabeth in her piercing canary jumper once again.

What horrified me the most was the way Elizabeth's flesh disappeared in the last months of cancer treatment. Though she was only a year older, Elizabeth had always been so much bigger than me, that I had to wait two years for her hand-me-downs. She had been so much stronger that she could hold me down and tickle me helpless until I peed. In the end, she could no longer stand, and her pajamas hung gaping from her shoulders. The muscles in her limbs had faded away.

A memory of the pastor's wife looms inside my head. She bent her kind pouted face sympathetically to my six-year-old level where I stood beside my parents at the funeral home, shaking hands. "Elizabeth is flying with the angels now," she said. But I hardly cared what some airy-light image of Elizabeth was doing among the clouds. I wanted to know where all those pounds of flesh had disappeared to. The heavy muscles that had tackled me and held me to the earth. They had been alive too.

For years after Elizabeth's death, I longed for her, and

for dreams about the way she had really been, but neither came. The pale, floating cherub I tried to conjure had no relation to the sister I had known. All I could feel was the emptiness of the house and yard. Now, sinking into exhaustion, I feel Elizabeth as she was. Chunky, muddy glow, the wet metal smell of the garden hose in the early summer turning the ground soggy between our toes. She chases me because she can, always running fastest, slips on the mucky wet grass and catches my ankle to make me fall too. We are both giggling and covered with mud.

Some presence pulls me deeper, no longer Elizabeth's chubby hand. Her grinning face expands, as if she has stuck the flowing hose in her mouth and the water is pushing her cheeks out grotesquely until she has to let go. Only this gargoyle keeps expanding into the terrifying visage of the sculpture Coatlicue, livid with serpents and claws. She stands above her court, orchestrating the ritual of sacrifice about to take place. A vivid enactment of legends I had studied so much, without ever knowing their truth. They parade in celebration, drumming and contorting ecstatically, before lying down to be cut open, their hearts torn out, still beating from the frenzied dance, and tossed among dried ears of corn from the previous harvest. The strange alchemy of spring offerings begins, sprouting and blooming from the gory mess before the blood has dried. The queen slices a vein, spouting her own blood until she is weak and fainting. And I am she, spinning into deep red darkness, weaving towards the light. Blood pouring and pouring out visions I cannot quite see. Then my belly begins to swell rapidly.

The sun stings like lemon juice in my eyes when I awake I am surprised by the young, naïve and sudden morning just moments after the darkness inside my head was engulfing me. Aria is already up running back and forth through the house in her pajamas. I catch her and carry her to her room to get dressed. When I pull the straps of her jumper over her shoulders, they strain and refuse to fasten. "They're too small!" I am astonished. They fit her only last week. Aria is growing and she giggles with delight.

Eric is quiet and intense at breakfast and frowns frequently, as if in response to an argument going on in his head. I do not interrupt; I let him leave without a goodbye. The heat is already rolling in humid waves. I take Aria outside early. From the back porch I watch her pushing an empty swing, squealing with happiness. Every once in a while she stops and stands with her back to me, whispering in conspiracy with the air.

The phone rings. A glance at my watch tells me it is recess time at school, it has got to be Eric. I stand with the phone at the window, where I can still keep an eye on Aria.

"We have to make a decision quickly," Eric says, his tone strangely warm and conciliatory. "That travel agent I spoke to found us a really good deal on plane tickets. Almost half price. But we'd have to leave next weekend, as soon as school's out."

I cough. Aria climbs the back porch and punches the latch on the screen door several times before coordinating it with her pull and opening it. The sound sparks through me, enlivening memories of Elizabeth and myself banging the back door the same way. "Can I think about it?"

"He can only hold the tickets until tomorrow. He'll need an answer."

"Till tomorrow then?"

Eric pauses. I can hear how he is weighing impatience

and calm. He controls the urgency he feels in order to convince me. He really wants this. "Okay. Please." He waits for several seconds, then hangs up.

Aria stands beside me. "Mom, can I have a cookie?"

"I'm surprised you're hungry, you ate such a big breakfast." It is easiest to mask my concern with small talk.

"It's not for me," she shrugs and gestures out towards the swings.

I give her two cookies and follow her out. I hardly see the snacks disappear before she turns back and begins unwinding the hose from its holder on the back wall. "It's hot," she says.

It is. I watch her and envy the worrilessness with which she soaks her clothes and dirties her feet. She unravels the hose carefully and turns the water on full blast, fitting her tiny thumb over the end so that the water flies further. Laughing loudly, she runs and shrieks, spraying the air in front of her. She runs until the hose reaches its limit. The smell of wet steamy earth is overwhelming.

She plays until the sun reaches its peak, and I call her in. I will have to get her some new clothes for this trip. We will go shopping after lunch.

DRIVING FOR JESUS

"Have you heard the good news about the Lord Jesus Christ?" The man in the back seat leans forward so far that his face sticks between the head rests, and his big red hands are flat against the front seat.

Roland hates talking about God. But after a year of taxiing, it is still the topic of choice among his fares. "I've heard everything," Roland says.

"Ah, cynicism," the man chuckles, "if there ever was a cry for help!"

"The only thing I need help with is paying the rent," Roland mutters.

"You know what the Lord Jesus Christ would say about that?" The man smacks the seat for emphasis. "He'd say, consider the lilies, they toil not, neither do they spin."

"So I should stop working?"

"It's a question of attitude. You got to trust in the Lord, and he will provide."

"Yeah, yeah. I'll get a check in the mail, will I?"

"Hard of heart!" The man's laugh becomes a cluttered smoker's cough. "You must accept Christ as your saviour or not only will you not be able to pay the rent, you'll burn forever in hell."

"I'm already in hell," Roland says, but the man does not hear. He is busy unleashing a tirade of fiery warnings and condemnation. He punctuates his rant with a good punch to the back of the driver's seat.

"Hey!" Roland screeches to a halt. "If you're going to damage my cab, you get out! How do I know you're not going to punch me next? This is why drivers are getting barriers between front and back, because of people like you."

"I wasn't going to punch you," the man says, holding his big palms up on either side of his florid face. "I'm just trying to spread the good news about the Saviour."

Roland glances at the man in the rear view mirror before pulling back into traffic.

Consider the lilies, Roland thinks. He ought to try that on Father Phil, when his next payment is due. Father Phil gave up all his spiritual possessions to become a taxi tycoon. But he retained his title, like Princess Diana after her divorce. Father Land-Phil, his employees like to call him, because that is where all their profits get dumped, and nothing is ever recycled. Whenever one of his drivers gets stabbed or robbed and they ask for expensive Plexiglas shields, Phil says, "We don't need more barriers in this society. What we need is more prayer!"

"What do I have to do to get money from Jesus?" Roland asks.

"Trust in him!" the man booms with equal emphasis on each word. "Why do you worry? You have your life and a job and you could have your faith."

"You think this is a good job?" Roland asks. "It's a damned dangerous job. Last week, one of my friends was beaten up, for fifty dollars. Beaten unconscious. I know two who have been stabbed in the last month. And the money, you know, sometimes I go all night with only two fares, but I've still got to pay my boss the same amount for the car. And then there are the people who don't pay."

The man in the back is silent. Roland looks at him suspiciously, then pulls over again. "Do you have money?"

"No," the man replies.

"So who's going to pay me?" Roland demands.

"Mary."

"Jesus H. Christ! Are you trying to tell me that Mary is going to appear on the hood of the car in a blue haze and hand over some bills? What are you, a saint?" Roland hollers. He does not usually yell so loudly, but the man's blusters have raised the tenor of the whole evening.

"Mary's my wife," the man says. "She'll pay when you get me home."

Roland does not know whether to believe him, but he is embarrassed after his outburst, so he pulls away from the curb once again.

*

Felicia used to feel sorry for the people who did not have enough to pay. She would ride with Roland on Saturday nights, although it meant he could not take groups of more than three. She did not like to stay home alone, and she thought it was fascinating. If someone could not pay, she would listen to their excuse with genuine sympathy, then apologize for expecting payment. Felicia also tipped too much in restaurants, even if it meant giving up her last dollar. She said it was a code of understanding among waitresses.

Roland experiences a pang with these memories. He vowed he would not think about Felicia, especially not when he is already in a bad mood. I would not tip a driver at all if I ever took a cab, he thinks. Everybody has fucked me over, why shouldn't I do the same to him?

Since Felicia moved out, he had developed a system.

"You know what this is?" Roland asks, holding up a small spiral notebook for the man in the back to see.

"What is that?"

"Whenever someone doesn't pay me, I write down their address. Then I go back there."

"Do they pay?"

"Some, but most don't," Roland says. "My new policy is that they give me some kind of collateral before they get out of the car. They have to pay to get it back."

"What do they give you?"

"Whatever they have. Watches, jackets, one man gave me an electric toothbrush. Yesterday, a woman gave me her shoes."

"Nice shoes?"

"Yeah, expensive."

Designer shoes, but no coat. Never trust a lone woman without a proper coat, Roland thinks. She talked about God as well. "Have you ever had a religious experience?" she asked him. "I don't just mean confirmation, or baptism or whatever, I mean something out of the blue."

For some reason Roland remembered the time he only pretended to put his quarters into the collection bag at church, pocketing them instead. The minister appeared to address the entire sermon directly to him after that. A sermon about greed. Somehow, Roland believed, God had whispered in the Reverend's ear what the guilty boy had just done.

"I was just sitting in that bar, when everything suddenly faded into the background, and I had a vision. It was a woman, a very kind, goddess woman, holding out her arms to me. It made me feel warm all over," the woman with no coat said.

Roland glanced at her in his mirror. She did not look

very warm. Her arms pudged out below the tight, short spandex sleeves, like a child's arms. Maybe she was a child. Even in the dark, he could see the goose bumps.

If Felicia were here, she would coax the girl up to the front seat with us, and rub her arms to warm her up, Roland thought. Then the three of them would drive around all night, offering "Party Rides." Roland could charge more for the privilege, except that Felicia would pardon most of the debts. The truth is, the girl looked a bit like Felicia.

"When I saw this woman," the girl in the back seat continued. "I knew I simply had to see my mother. No matter what, I just had to get to her whatever way I could."

No matter what, Roland thought. He noticed that the girl did not have a purse either. But they had already reached the address she had given him.

"I think this is it," she said, peering out.

What kind of mother lives over a bar on Queen Street, Roland wondered. He waited.

"I don't have any money," the girl finally said, sliding towards the door.

"What do you have?" Roland demanded. If Felicia had stayed, he would have Father Phil and his thugs after him for the huge debt he would have incurred. Roland wondered whether Father Phil would accept his cache of collateral for payment. The trunk was half-full. It made Roland think of the great pile of crutches and canes collected at a cathedral he had visited in Quebec City. People had left them after experiencing miracles. He imagined accepting someone's crutch as payment. Driving for Jesus, a miraculous free ride.

The girl was busy looking herself up and down for

something to leave. "My shoes?" she held up a yellow leather pump.

"Fine," Roland said. "You get them back when you pay."

She handed him the pumps, then pattered across the sidewalk in her nyloned feet. Roland waited to see if anyone answered her knock, and was a little surprised when someone did. After the door closed behind her, he wrote down the address. He knew it was unlikely that he would get any money by returning. Just another door slammed in his face by an angry boyfriend. Or maybe her mother really did live there.

If you are not getting any money, you might as well return the shoes, a voice spoke in his head. He knew that voice. She would also tell him to apologize. Maybe he would, and maybe the girl would go for another ride with him.

*

"Just up here," the man in the back seat points to a house. "This is where I live." The house he is pointing to is dark. "So just give me a minute and I'll be out to pay you." He reaches for the door.

"Wait!" Roland yells. "How do I know you're going to come back? You might just go inside and stay there."

"I swear by Jesus' name, on the Holy Bible!" he says.

Roland snorts. "You have a bible here?"

The man pats his pockets. "I usually have one, but I don't have anything on me tonight. Not even a watch."

"Let me see your shoes," Roland says. The man lifts his foot to reveal a muddy, rotting sneaker.

"The only thing I've got is the shirt on my back," he says.

Roland scrunches his nose in distaste at the sweaty shirt, but he motions to the man to give it to him. The man sighs deeply and undoes the buttons which are tight over his protruding stomach. He hands Roland the smelly shirt and climbs out of the car. Roland watches as he approaches and knocks on the front door. There is no answer. He looks in some windows and disappears around the back for a few minutes. Finally, he walks back to the curb and leans on Roland's window.

"Sorry, man. Seems Mary's out tonight," he says.

Roland rolls his eyes in disgust. "I should have made you get out back there."

"Hey," the big man says. "It's kind of chilly out, and I have to wait for Mary to come home. Can I have my shirt back?"

Roland laughs. "Jesus will keep you warm!" He stuffs the dirty shirt under his seat and drives away.

THE TROUBLE WITH HEAVEN

My parents always told me that I had red hair because I was born during a heat wave. I was thirteen before I realized that was a joke. Ever since, I have been wondering, what else is? It is ridiculously hot for the end of May, and the bus is sweating with the fever of thirty restless teenagers a month away from high school graduation. The driver yells whenever someone sticks an arm or head out a window, but somehow the limbs keep slipping out into the wind of their own accord. I used to look at my baby pictures and pity the red-skinned, fuzzy headed thing, imagining the waves of fire scorching her face. That is what I feel like now.

When we reach Camp Nazareth, the lake offers little hope of relief. A thick glaze of brown-green algae holds the surface still with hardly a lap against the beach. We gather around our teacher, Mr. Van Wyk, and a camp counselor with "Jesus Saves!" emblazoned in neon across her T-shirt. They call out room assignments, and direct us to the cabins which encircle the large retreat centre.

"Damn," Vanessa mutters when she hears we have been designated bunkmates. She shakes back her water coloured hair, and rolls her grey eyes. She grabs her bag and huffs up the hill without waiting for me.

Vanessa and I are cousins. A stretchable silvery cord joins my right temple to her left, has since we were toddlers. We used to walk around the playground of the

Christian elementary school warning our classmates not to trip on our invisible link.

"You're a ball and chain!" Vanessa says when I enter the cabin behind her.

"You'll be rid of me for good soon," I say. I received my acceptance to the University of Toronto just two days ago. Vanessa has not decided what she will do once we graduate. She has been too busy, desperately courting some of the cooler kids all year, determined to join their ranks before it is too late. My bizarre reputation is hampering her efforts.

The cabin door opens. Pat and Lena, both decidedly unpopular, come in and place their bags on the other set of bunk beds.

"Oh, great!" Vanessa says, rolling her eyes again. She tosses her stuff on the bottom bunk and leaves, easily picking up the trail of cigarette smoke into the woods.

After supper the counselors build a fire for everyone to gather around while the sun goes down. I do not try to approach Vanessa, instead I sit as near as I can to Peter. I have decided I may want to fall in love with him. He is tall with dark hair, and always dresses in black pants and a white cotton shirt, unlike the other guys in shorts and T-shirts. He hangs out with a small, skinny guy named Clay, and no one else. If only I can be fascinating enough, I think, I might persuade Peter to like me.

Counselors with guitars place themselves at three sides of the fire, leaving one as a chimney. The smoke rises with the songs about seeking God's kingdom, grasping at the love of Christ. Reaching for the moon. The smoke wavers and dissipates well before the tallest tree tops. Then that urgent, chilling verse:

You can't change your mind,
you don't know the date,
Christ comes like a thief, and it's too late,
too late, for those left behind.

Two people on a hill, a fiery chariot like a bolt of lightning swoops one away, leaves the other alone with nothing but dread. I picture this every time I hear that song. What if they are lovers, best friends, a relationship wronged for eternity?

I shudder and realize that the group around the fire has broken up. We have been given an hour before lights out. I glimpse Vanessa heading towards the exclusive cigarette pit, and walk alone to the cabin. I try to read, but Pat and Lena return and chatter noisily. I switch off the light on my side and move my pillow to the foot of my bunk where there is a small window. Dots of light flicker occasionally in the darkness, fire-flies or cigarette butts, I do not know which. I pretend to be asleep when Vanessa comes in and bangs around in the little bathroom.

We used to share dreams, literally, whenever we slept in the same room. We would write down what we remembered as soon as we woke up, then compare. They often matched. But when Vanessa lies down on the bunk below, I can feel her resentment like a massive plank between us. There will not be any unconscious communication between us tonight. Lucky for Vanessa, because sometime later, in the middle of the pitchest black, I awake sweating and shaking. I have just dreamt of a massive light bursting through the woods and blaring in the little window. My head is still at the foot, outside there is not a flicker. I turn myself around on the bed, but my nerves continue to jump.

When I was younger I used to lie awake, staring obsessively at my bedroom window. The room was at the front of the house, and though there was little traffic, the occasional car headlights would tighten my veins and set my heart pounding. No matter how I assured myself it was just a passing car, there was always that moment when the white light filling the room seemed too bright, so sudden that I knew it had to be Jesus returning, with a terrifying nuclear glare. Why should I be afraid if I know I am one of the chosen? The words of the song turn endlessly in my head. It is too late, too late for those left behind.

*

Vanessa groans when a counselor announces that our canoeing partners will be the same as our bunkmates. My night was restless after the dream, and I am too groggy to care. I climb unsteadily into one end and try to balance while Vanessa climbs in the other. The counselors give a short lesson on how to steer then lead us off, cutting through the algae surface. Vanessa and I struggle, wiggling the boat side to side, we cannot coordinate our efforts enough to move steadily forward. Soon the rest of the flotilla is well ahead of us. Only Peter and Clay are as far behind as we are, not because of any difficulty, but deliberately avoiding the pack. They pull up beside us. Peter's black pants must be hot in the sun, I think. He is smiling right at me.

"Need a hand?" he asks and grabs the side of our canoe to give us a push. The boat rocks wildly.

"Don't!" Vanessa shrieks. I laugh.

"You're not going anywhere like that," Clay says.

"We should switch," Peter says. "Holly get in the boat

with me, and Clay take her place. Then at least one person in each boat will know what they're doing."

I am so eager to comply that I stand up and step into the next boat before anything is steady. Both canoes flip, sending all four of us into the murky lake. Despite my life-jacket, I go under, and for several seconds do not know which way is up. Then a strong arm around my waist sets me straight. My feet touch mush, and I realize the water is only chest deep. Peter holds me against him, I can feel his leg through our wet clothes. "You okay?" he asks.

I cough and smile. Vanessa screams. "Idiots! You fucking losers!" Her face is coated in slime which gives her skin an ocean tinge. She wades frantically to the beach, like a furious mermaid who has suddenly grown feet.

*

After supper, the counselors lead us into the woods and along a path that goes steeply uphill. In the deepening twilight, everything develops an ethereal quality, except the mosquitoes. I feel like I can step off the path at any moment, and slip between worlds. Peter walks directly ahead of me; I decide to stay.

"Welcome to the Eagle's Nest," someone announces. Eventually, I can see the dark wood structure through the purplish light.

"I've heard they found this building here before they built the camp," Peter says close to my ear. "No one knows what it was for."

It is a triangular structure with a huge window overlooking the lake. The counselors have tried to make it chapelish with rows of benches and some felt banners proclaiming the love of Christ. But they have failed to take away the mysterious feel to the place. The counselor who is also a pastor stands up with his back to the window which now frames a dramatic orange sunset. He begins with a prayer, then a mini-sermon.

He bellows exuberance and enthusiasm. I blur my eyes and watch him dance like a little black stick person in front of a field of fire. By the time he finishes, the room is nearly black. Then somebody walks up and flicks on harsh lights.

"Now to continue my topic of communicating with God, we're going to play a communication game," the pastor says. "Charades."

He counts us off into groups of five. I am delighted to find Peter in mine. Vanessa looks over longingly because Mark, her latest object of desire, and Jacqueline, the most popular girl in the class join us. Lena is the fifth. The pastor instructs us to choose a Biblical story or concept and portray it in mime while the rest of the class guesses.

No one in our group has any suggestions. Finally I say, "I know, the second coming."

Jacqueline rolls her eyes. "We can't do that!"

"It was good when the sun was setting, the lake of fire, it would have been a perfect backdrop," I say. Peter chuckles, so I continue. "We could interpret hell as black emptiness." I gesture towards the window which now reflects everything back inside.

"As if," Jacqueline says.

"Anyone have any other suggestions?" I ask. They are silent.

"What do we do for hell? A wild, sinful party?" Peter says grinning.

"An orgy," Mark contributes. They grab their guts with laughter.

"I was thinking more of people on a hill, Jesus shows up, some get taken and some are left behind. Like the song," I say. The others shrug and wait. "You know what I don't get?" I continue. "What happens if you are chosen, but you love someone who is left behind?"

"I never thought of that," Peter says.

"If you love them, that's why you try and convert them," Jacqueline says.

"What if they don't?" I ask.

"That's not your responsibility," Mark says.

"It's not a question of responsibility," I say, feeling agitated. "How can I be happy in heaven when someone I love is damned?" Jacqueline looks disturbed. Her habitual contempt has disappeared and she is actually listening to me. I want to tell her more.

"I think if you are chosen, it's not possible to really love someone who is damned," Lena says.

Peter and I both begin to protest. The pastor interrupts. "Five more minutes!"

We have not even begun to rehearse, everyone frowns. We quickly divide ourselves up. Mark will be Christ, Jacqueline and Lena his angels. It is a coin toss between Peter and me and I lose. I will be damned.

The other groups begin, most with easy, obvious skits. Adam and Eve playing up their horror at discovering their nakedness. Everyone laughs. Our charade comes last. The scene is awkward and unclear as the heavenly troupe appears to take Peter away, leaving me alone on the stage to depict my hellish pain. I sink to my knees, clasping my hands in the air, then I rub at my eyes and pull at my hair. The audience stares blankly, no one offers any guesses. I must look ridiculous, to the audience and to anyone lurking in the dark forest below. A lunatic, literally, with crazy fire hair waving her arms as if to the moon. Nobody understands. I feel myself sweating and blushing deeply. Finally, Peter sneaks behind me and pokes me in the bum with a blackboard pointer. The audience gasps and giggles. "It's a pitchfork!" Peter explains, and they laugh. We are the only group who has failed to convey our concept.

I have made an utter fool of myself. Even as we file out, the heat hovers around my face, which still matches the colour of my hair. But to my surprise, I have had another effect. Jacqueline approaches me outside the Eagle's Nest, clearly upset. Maybe she loves someone we do not know about. Mark stands behind her. "What do you think?" she asks. "About heaven? About what happens when we die?"

"There's a lot more to it than what they tell us," I say mysteriously. The counselors interrupt, pushing us down the path to the cabins.

Jacqueline persists. "I'm freaked out, Holly. You freaked us all out. I won't be able to sleep."

Vanessa appears suddenly at my elbow, astonished to see Jacqueline and Mark talking to me. Peter walks just ahead. "Meet me later then," I whisper, and something shivers over my body. The thrill of knowing something they do not. Something fascinating. We quickly decide to sneak out once everyone else is asleep, and meet again at the base of the Eagle's Nest path.

*

"What's going on?" Vanessa hisses when we are back in the cabin getting ready for bed.

I smile knowingly and tilt my head towards Pat and

Lena. "Just keep your clothes handy," I say lowly so the others won't hear.

The darkness feels prickly with excitement. My heart and limbs jump. I can feel Vanessa tugging anxiously at my temple, but she does not speak. We have to wait for Pat's rattley snore, and when it finally comes, we slip out of our beds and back into the night. Peter and Clay are already waiting by the path, Peter's white shirt the only thing visible against the backdrop of trees. Luckily, he carries a tiny flashlight, something I did not think of.

"Are you sure Mark and Jacqueline are coming?" Vanessa whispers.

I shrug. At this point, I do not really care. I stand close enough to Peter to feel his shirt sleeve brush against my arm.

A rustling of footsteps approaches. "It's them!" Vanessa says. Peter shines his flashlight. Lena. "What are you doing here?" Vanessa demands.

"I heard you guys leave," Lena says.

Vanessa kisses her teeth and steps back away from the rest of us to wait. Finally, Mark and Jacqueline approach together. Vanessa is too happy to see Mark to notice just how closely together.

Peter leads the way with his flashlight. The path is steep and difficult in the dark. When I stumble, Peter reaches back offering his hand. He helps me past a hard part, and keeps holding on. I am so happy that the mosquitoes do not bother to bite my bare legs. I hardly recognize the trip from earlier, maybe because the group behind me is silent, unlike the earlier boisterous crowd. Suddenly, the Eagle's Nest stands right in front of us, exceedingly dark.

"Do you think it's locked?" I whisper. We feel our way

along a wall to the door. Peter pushes it open, and we file inside.

"I'll turn off the flashlight," Peter says. "The big window is visible from below."

"Somebody will report mysterious lights tomorrow," I say. "They'll think it's haunted."

"They already say this place is haunted, don't they?" Clay says.

"What!" Vanessa and Jacqueline in unison.

"That's exactly what we need," I say. "A ghost. To answer all our questions." Peter still holds my hand in the dark. A point of fear prickles at the base of my skull, but the knowledge that the others are more afraid than I am makes me bold. There is a thrilling activity in the air, which no longer smells of insect repellent. Maybe it really is haunted.

"What exactly are we doing here?" Vanessa asks quietly. There is tension in her voice, as in the air, tension between fear and the desire to impress.

"Let's hold a séance," I say. There are several seconds of strained silence. I am aware that any one of them could now take the initiative to refuse and quickly sway everyone else. He or she would have to take that step.

Instead, Mark snorts and says, "This ought to be good. What do we do? Sit in a circle and hold hands?"

Perfect, I think. We all sit cross-legged. My left knee slides slightly under Peter's and he rests our clasped hands on my thigh. Vanessa sits to my right and takes my hand, happy for any human contact, happier probably to have Mark on her right.

"Who are we going to contact?" Peter asks.

"Do we know anyone who died recently?" I ask.

"There was this guy," Jacqueline says. "My neighbour.

He crashed his car last summer and passed away. Todd."

"Todd what?" I ask.

"I don't know if this is a good idea," Jacqueline back-tracks.

I have my own doubts. How much can this Todd really know about the nature of heaven and hell? Unless death grants you instant wisdom. "Don't you want to know where he is?" I ask.

"I don't know. He wasn't a Christian or anything."

"Then he's in hell, obviously," Lena says.

Shut up, I think.

"He might be able to communicate with us," I say.

"If he is in hell, I'll feel like shit for eternity," Jacqueline says.

"It's not your fault," Mark says. Jacqueline does not respond.

"Just sit quietly and concentrate. Think about Todd," I say. Vanessa's hand is wet with sweat that seems to be conducting bolts of tense energy back and forth between us. My left hand in Peter's is being drawn ever so slowly up my leg. Halfway along my thigh, he lets go of my hand and continues to move his own.

"Try to keep your mind open to any kind of communication." I am fumbling for things to say. Peter fingers the hem of my shorts then slides his hand under.

"Todd?" My voice cracks. "If you are here, give us a sign."

Peter slowly rubs his finger against the bit of cotton panties between my legs. I shiver. Vanessa shifts uncomfortably. My grip tightens on her hand.

"Listen . . . for any sound," I say and pray they cannot hear the blood pounding through my veins. Peter slips his fingers inside my panties. Somebody else say something, I think. Please, anybody, Lena, Todd. "Todd?" I say out loud. I have to move; I shudder and jump. Peter pulls his hand away and Vanessa stands up screaming.

"What's wrong with you? Are you possessed?"

"Where are the lights?" Jacqueline says. "Mark, find the lights!"

I hug my legs to my chest while the others pat along the walls for a light switch. Please don't let them find it, I think. I do not want Peter to see my face.

With the commotion we do not hear the crunch of twigs breaking, the approach of footsteps through the woods. We do not hear them enter the cabin. When the lights of two powerful flashlights flood the room, Jacqueline screams.

"What's going on here?" Mr. Van Wyk and the pastor scan the room with their flashlights, looking perhaps for bottles or discarded clothes, but find nothing.

"Let's go," Mr. Van Wyk says. "We'll discuss your punishment back at school tomorrow."

*

I stay in bed in the morning while Vanessa, Pat and Lena head off for breakfast. "Tell them I don't feel well," I say. They pretend not to hear. When they return after breakfast to pack, Vanessa looks at me coldly.

"Don't even think of trying to sit beside me on the bus."

I continue stuffing clothes into my bag and say nothing.

"Everyone thinks you're demented!" she says.

"Why? Because I don't believe everything they tell me?"

Vanessa shakes her head and smiles at the air in front of her. "In fact, don't even try speaking to me," she says.

I point to my temple. "What about the cord?"

"The cord?" Vanessa lifts her hand with two fingers spread like a pair of scissors to her left temple. Snip! I feel the cut like a bolt of lightning through my nervous system. "Grow up!" Vanessa says. She slams the cabin door open and runs to the bus to get a good seat.

I reach the bus last; only the front seats are empty, which is fine with me. I can lean against the window facing no one. I am aware that Peter must be somewhere behind me in the bus, but I will not look. Vanessa too. An ache stretches out from my head, the severed stump of cord tingling like a phantom limb. Vanessa and I will likely never sleep in the same room again, never share another dream or nightmare.

As the bus pulls out through the Huntsville rocks and woods, the grate of teenaged voices melds into one loud, buzzing din. I doze off and on while the trees give way to open fields. This is likely my last trip on a yellow school bus ever. In the fall it will be replaced by Toronto's subways and streetcars. My world will expand exponentially. And when people ask where I got this bright red hair, I'll tell them I had a narrow escape from a hot blast of heaven.

FIRE, EARTH AND FORTUNE COOKIES

He kept every Chinese cookie fortune he ever received. Fortunes from towns and suburbs around the country. Cookies from restaurants where every dish came with chicken balls and fluorescent red sauce. He put every one in his wallet until it bulged like a boy's pocketful of cherished stones, then emptied it haphazardly one night into a pig-shaped cookie jar I'd had since I was a child. It was the last thing he did before he left in February. It was New Year's Eve. The lunar, Chinese New Year, but he did not know that. He is not Chinese, he just likes the food.

"That'll lighten the load," he said, replacing his wallet and balancing his guitar and his back-pack.

"Why do you have to leave me alone here?" I asked again.

"You can come with me!" he said, his eyes belligerent and blue. There was no use explaining to him again that leaving was really leaving and not paying the rent. There would be no place to come back to, except a friend's living room floor. He would have said, "So what? We've done it before." We have, many times, and I cannot do it even once more. There are plants to water.

*

When Spring comes, heaven will rain happiness on you.

*

Every day of his absence I will choose one fortune to read and ponder. I give the pig a good shaking first, so that when I choose, it will be either intuition or pure randomness that guides my fingers. I have set the pig up on my dresser like an altar, with candles and incense. A shrine to him that might draw him back. I add small mementos, his broken watch, a bit of toenail from beside the tub.

Each time I choose a fortune, I place it in a small pile beside the jar instead of returning it. I would not want to pull the same one again and repeat my fate.

*

His voice inflamed me. Like a billowing tenor, but with a salty female timbre. Unlike any other. His fingers focused on the strings of his burnished guitar. His eyes wandered over and pinned me in the crowd. Lucky one, while the others drifted away. What got into me? The flame in an opal, the fly in an ice cube. He got into me and I closed up around.

It was remarkable, how I came to be in a too smoky club that hot June night. So unlikely, that our coupling seems less surprising in retrospect. Twist of fate, twist of words, a homonym. Some co-workers asked me to meet them at *Evening Fair*. I only agreed to go because it was somebody's birthday. Too unsophisticated to know its location, I turned up at *Night Fare* which was considerably murkier than the popular night club where I was expected. I sat down anyway and ordered myself some beer.

His eyes penetrated the blinding spotlight and found me. He stabbed me with a look and hooked me with a tone. He approached me where I was clinging alone to a cocktail table top no bigger than a plate.

"You look so cold and pretty," he said and sat. Then drawing an intimate finger across my cheek leaving his sweat, he asked, "Is it powder?"

"No. It's a state."

He laughed and stayed and bought himself a drink. The evening continued like a rare piece of music, assured of the next note, though I could never get a hold of the melody. I would have drifted into sleep, but someone slammed into our table and drenched me with cold beer.

"Your dress!" He jumped up. "Let me take you home. I'll rinse it for you." I mutely agreed while he found a cab. The stars must have been overworking that night because not a block away the cab swerved to avoid a drunken reveler (the same one who had fallen into our table?) and turned head on into a reeking dumpster.

"Two accidents mean a sure thing," he said and kissed me in the crashed cab. I did not tell him there had been three.

*

Why couldn't I go with him? I tried to explain but he shrugged off every reason. Now I am here alone with all the time to try and understand for myself.

When I was a child in elementary school, I thought of the playground as a giant pinball machine. The other kids rushed about like frantic balls in the game. Energetic, spring-fired, fighting gravity. I was a pin for them to bounce off and ignore. Those were long playground days, but I was never bored watching.

One swampy recess after a rain, I literally became

rooted to the pinball machine. I stood still so long, in my rain boots, in the mud, that I sank and stuck. I knew it was happening, but I would not move. I was fascinated by the slow, determined drawing of the earth, and the faint suction enveloping my feet. I watched my toes disappear, my heels become anchored. I smiled knowingly at the row of measly trees beside the fence.

When the bell rang, I was less satisfied with my situation, but it was too late. Everyone else filed inside, then stood at the classroom windows pointing and laughing. A teacher had to come back outside and lift me back to freedom and to all the taunting kids.

*

Sometimes what you want most is not what you most need.

*

He stayed the night. He stayed the week. He never got around to washing my dress, and he never asked me why I had been there alone, wobbling on a tippy chair, chilled in a hot and gyrating room. When I asked him where he lived, he pointed to his feet. I was charmed, and awkwardly attended every gig, sitting with other friends of the band who knew how to rock and move to the music unselfconsciously. I sat on my fingers, so no one wondered why they were not moving. Usually, I did not know anyone's name. The music was too loud for introductions.

I sat there waiting, hating the dense smoke, but loving the flame that finally stepped out on stage. I could endure smugly because I knew there was a special current between me and that spark. All these other people swaying and posturing as if they knew. I knew he was singing for me.

And when the shows increased in stature and frequency, I sped up too. Every night if I had to. Even if it meant cursing out of bed just a few hours later (while he slept) with raspy red eyes. Finding my way to where the temp agency had assigned my next gig. Twice I went to the wrong identical office building in my exhaustion. At one, they put me to work sealing envelopes for a day and a half before I learned I was in the wrong place. The days were as dense and hazy as the ugly night bars.

It all led up to the big road trip. I had to go along. His words, really. He said I was his inspiration, his face in the crowd. And I knew I could not let the fire go out of my life. I had to go.

*

Why did I crave that fire? Is it obvious? A simple truth that we all accept in lieu of explanation? Just "it's love," or "it's fear." I was attracted like the proverbial moth to the flame, where I knew I could not remain. But I did not know. I had always thought maybe I could. The little girl on the playground watched the feisty players with longing. I envied the red-faced, flying-haired girls. I imagined what it might be like to be them, to possess their motion. Meanwhile, my feet stayed put, and I was too afraid to approach. But I always harboured the secret hope that one day one of them might approach me, see something in me to which they might connect.

It did not happen until that night when he touched my cheek and sent a bolt of electricity through me. We became for a while a closed circuit, ungrounded, where lightning is most deadly.

*

A girlfriend is a bottle of wine, a wife an empty bottle.

*

He gave me the best corner of the van, except after each performance when I was the least tired, or had the least excuse to be, and I drove. He held up a towel to shield me from the band so I could change my underwear. He was never so callous as to suggest I should not care. The trip was tense and exhilarating. He was on top of the world, and to top it all off, when we reached the west coast, he married me. A hasty ceremony at Vancouver's city hall. There was no reception. We had to have the van back to Al's brother in Toronto in a week. We left the hall and started driving.

We saved our celebration until I had found us a basement apartment in Toronto and we moved in. He chose a Chinese restaurant. "For sentimental value," he said. The food was closer to authentic, but the fortune cookies were something else.

"A wife is an empty bottle," I read. "That's disgusting. They can't print fortunes like that!"

He laughed heartily. "It's great," he said. "It's funny."

"I'm serious. I'm going to go and tell the manager he should buy his fortunes from another company. It's offensive."

"I'm sure he'll heed your advice immediately," he said.

I scowled and kissed my teeth at his ugly sarcasm.

"Lighten up!" he said.

I would not. I was angry. By the time we reached home in silence, he was pissed off too. He sat up watching television all night, though our apartment is all one room, and I had to work in the morning.

*

The agency has run out of temp positions for now. So I stay inside, I stay in my pajamas, I eat tinned food. The snow piles up against the two small windows so that only a crack of daylight can creep in along the tops. I imagine it piling up in the outside stairwell, blocking the door, my fire escape. The basement floor bludgeons my feet with its iciness, boring through my flimsy slippers. As much as possible, I stay in my bed.

He always slept naked. His body hot and incessant like an electric blanket. He heated the bed and the whole basement with his bare feet. Now I have piled every blanket and sweater around me, even the old sleeping bag that despite several washings, still smells like our van trip.

*

Every man is a volume if you know how to read him.

*

Between the sheets. This was his favourite party trick. He would announce that everyone must read their fortunes aloud and add the words "between the sheets" at the end. It was a good joke, if there was someone new at the table, especially if it was someone timid, whose ears turned easily pink. He particularly enjoyed the game on our trip. Speaking too loudly in small town family Chinese restaurants, where there was not a Chinese face in sight. He liked to flaunt sexual innuendoes because he was the only band member with his girlfriend along. He would wink or raise an eyebrow at me and I would giggle, while the others, who all had girlfriends back in Toronto, just rolled their eyes or flicked their cigarettes. If the shows were going well, we would splurge and get ourselves a separate motel room.

*

The landlord is pounding on the door. I know it is him because I heard his footsteps upstairs go outside and around. I crouch in the bathtub and pull the shower curtain to hide myself. A key turns in the lock.

"Shouldn't you wait till they're home?" a woman's voice asks.

"Look, I told you, they're away. I haven't heard a peep from down here in weeks. Who knows when they'll be back? I need those sockets now," the landlord says. Just inside the entrance way is a combination locked door that leads to a crawl space under the back porch. Storage space that the landlord still uses. He twirls the lock and crawls in.

"They can't have been gone that long," the woman says. "Look, they left a candle burning."

"What?" his voice is muffled until he crawls back out. "Holy shit! They're gonna burn the house down!" He stomps across the room to extinguish the candle on my altar. He pauses there. "Will you look at this, Marge?"

"What is it?" she crosses the room as well. "Shit, some kind of Voodoo set-up do you think?"

"I always knew that chick was weird, the way she stares at you?"

"We'd better leave before they come home."

They cross back to the door. "Burn us all in our beds," the landlord mutters and slams the door shut behind him. I wait a few minutes before climbing out of the tub. There are slushy footprints across the floor.

*

Beware of those who are not what they seem.

*

He accused me of deceiving him. "You used to be adventurous, remember?" I remember he once put me on the handlebars of his bike and steered me through traffic. I was too terrified to scream, and breathless when he finally let me off. He told me I looked stunning with my hair all wind-blown, then he kissed me in some unknown park where we had stopped.

He started watching afternoon talk shows, drumming the remote with frustration. After the road trip, the gigs petered out, because Al, the bass-player, went back to school. "Things'll pick up in the summer," I suggested. He threw the remote across the room.

"You can't just take an eight month break in this business. You've got to carry the momentum. All the contacts we made on this trip, we've got to follow through or people will forget about us. Got to keep moving."

All I gained from the trip were several pounds from greasy chicken balls, and an immense credit card debt.

*

I imagine his death. Something bizarre like an out of control cruise ship full of drunken carousers plowing into a wharf. He would be the sole casualty of the freak accident, crushed against the pillar of a river-side café where he was singing for tossed coins. His splintered guitar would be fished from the water, captured for the world on TV.

This is not just out of anger, but curiosity. What would it mean to end it all for once? Relief, release from the constant scramble for fuel to feed the desperate attachment, this desperate love. One last flame of pain. The pile of used fortunes on my dresser looks curiously like a fragile heap of twigs, ready to light, quickly to ash.

*

At Christmas I brought home a tiny pine tree in a pot. I did not want anything that had been cut and killed. I put it on our milk-crate table and attached a single foil star. When he came home he laughed and snarled at what he called my incipient domesticity.

The band had a New Year's party to play. When Al finished his exams they began practicing again for the first time in weeks. Rehearsals were not going well. The band was getting tired of his ultimatums.

"They just don't have the same drive that I have," he kept saying. "I'd be better off on my own." He soon was. The party was a disaster, and the band officially split.

*

There are no accidents, only fate.

*

I feed the tree dregs of thin cranberry tea. I have taken to reusing the bags several times so I will not run out. I do not want to have to go to the store for more. The colour is fainter with each cup, reminding me that Christmas is long over.

"Let's go," he said in January.

"How?" I asked. "We've got a year's lease here."

He snorted derisively. "A piece of paper."

"How would we survive?"

"I can busk on street corners. I'll get in touch with people, find a new band." He paced across the small basement, rattling random chords on his guitar, drowning my objections with noise.

Snow piled up against the basement windows. I imagined watching it melt and finding a place to plant the small pine outside, where it would get some sun.

A few weeks later he was ready to go.

"Where?" I asked.

"I don't know. I'll head south."

To New Orleans for Mardi Gras? And make me give you up for Lent? But I'm not Catholic.

*

The landlord is not home when my elbow knocks the candle off its base and its flame licks the flimsy scarf which covers the dresser top. I manage to smother it with the old sleeping bag, but not before it sets off the smoke detector. Not before the flames leap along the wall and leave permanent shadows of dark soot. I stand on my bed to snatch the screaming alarm from the ceiling and claw out the battery. Then quiet and listen. No frantic footsteps upstairs. No distant wail of sirens. Fortunate.

The altar has been immolated, the whole dresser top blackened. The clothes in the top drawer are scorched, and everything reeks of smoking acrylic sleeping bag fibres. I stuff all the burnt fabric into a garbage bag, but I will wait to set it on the curb till the landlord's suspicions ease.

In the bathroom, I stare in the mirror. My face is dark with ash. The bags under my eyes grown huge, like suitcases. So appropriate, it makes me smile. Sooty Persephone. She swallowed a seed from his pomegranate heart, and she will stay underground until someone rescues her. The phone rings. I know it is the temp agency, and not him, but this time I will answer it anyway.

SUNSPOTS

Her father is dead. That was the cause of the blue, cobwebby hazes hanging in the corners of Genevieve's room for the last week. The shadows are beginning to ebb now, leaving stark white walls in the face of the gloom having become a fact. Alice, the night counselor, woke her up just before seven to say Genevieve's mother was on the phone. Genevieve could tell that Alice already knew the bad news, because she stood by her side during the call, monitoring.

Alice follows her down the hall, leaving Genevieve alone only when she steps into the shower, turned fully hot, to steam up the bathroom like a humid summer's day. When Genevieve was small, her family always drove to the lake with a picnic lunch on the first hot weekend of each year. The summer when she was twelve sticks in her mind like wet tar on the soles of her feet. "You're supposed to be happy. It's beach day!" her mother said, snapping open the blinds in her bedroom. Her sister Christa had to drag Genevieve by the arm onto the floor.

The stretch of beach was already crowded with similar traditioners, and despite the humidity, the wind coming off Lake Huron was strong. The girls walked down to the water. "Hey!" their father hollered. "You're still dressed!" They had no intention of removing the T-shirts they wore over their self-conscious bathing suits.

"Why do I bother buying you bathing suits when you're just going to wear your clothes over top? Why aren't you wearing bikinis?" Gordon Williams badgered his daughters loudly enough to turn their ears pink. "Why aren't you out looking for some boys? Look, over there, playing frisbee."

Christa just rolled her eyes, but Genevieve would look out from behind her sunglasses, down the beach to the other teenagers. Attractive, and repellent, they existed in a world out of reach to her, a world of bright colours, tans and sun. She concentrated on the lake water spraying in her face.

Genevieve sneezes water from her nose. The shower is pouring down on her face, and someone is banging on the bathroom door. She grabs a towel just as Christa peeks in. There are no locks on any of the doors.

"Sorry, Gen," Christa says.

"I'll just be a minute." Genevieve dries quickly, then returns to her room. Christa's face is puffy and tired. Beautiful Christa with her white-light eyes and glinty blonde hair. Crying dulls her.

"How are you?" Christa asks.

Genevieve shrugs and dresses, then follows Christa downstairs to the car waiting at the curb with a woman behind the wheel. Genevieve stops. "You brought Tess?"

Christa turns angrily. "My father just died, Gen. I need Tess with me right now!" She gets into the passenger seat and slams the door, while Genevieve scuttles into the back.

"Hi, Gen. I'm very sorry about your father," Tess says, although the windows are open, and she must have heard what Genevieve said. Genevieve tries to thank her, but only clears her throat. Their meetings always begin this way, but the truth is, she envies Tess and Christa more than anyone can imagine.

After five minutes of silence, Christa sighs. "Tess is staying at a motel, so Mom doesn't have to worry," she says. She did not always plan to have Tess stay at a motel. The tense weekend when Christa first brought Tess home, she put their bags together in one bedroom. Genevieve washed the dishes while her parents held a conference in the kitchen.

"I don't think we should allow Christa to behave like this under our noses. It's not right," her mother said.

"You're not going to stop them," her father chuckled. He found the idea of Christa and Tess's sexual life amusing and faintly titillating. "They could just go back to their own apartment."

"That's not the point," her mother said. "If we allow it here, it's like we're giving our approval."

He laughed again. "They aren't waiting for our approval."

"I know that, but still."

"What harm can it do if they like to be in there together? We should send Genny in with them, give her some colour," he laughed. "You used to let them have slumber parties."

"That was different!"

"How do you know? Who knows what they did? All I remember is a lot of suspicious giggling."

*

The morning sun is stubborn and hot for May. When Genevieve steps into her mother's dim house, her eyes fill with spots, hovering shadows which refuse to fade. Her mother holds her arms out to both her daughters, while her cousin Scott, his wife Barbara, and numerous older neighbours and friends monitor the appropriateness of Genevieve's reactions.

Her dad always made an elaborate show of hugging, but to different ends. When his nephew first introduced his fiancée, Gordon hugged Barbara, then reached down and grabbed her by the buttocks.

"That's what we used to call a babysitter's hug!" he said when Barbara shrieked.

*

The house rustles with quiet condolences. Waiting. Waiting for the event to move into the past. Filling in the painful time with flowers and frozen casseroles. The clock chimes noon, and Genevieve opens the stereo cabinet.

"Gen, no, we don't need this!" Christa says.

Her father listened to the radio every Wednesday and Saturday at noon. The local station broadcast a sombre list of all those area residents who had died in the previous few days. As he got older, he became obsessed, he could not miss a name. In January he told Genevieve, "It won't be long now. They'll be saying mine." He would like to know I heard it, Genevieve thinks and stubbornly holds the dial.

After lunch, Scott and Barbara's three-year-old daughter asks loudly enough for all to hear, "Mom, where's Uncle Gordon?"

Barbara smiles. "Honey, Uncle Gordon is in heaven now with your grandpa."

"No, he's not," Samantha says. "He's right there, by the ceiling." She points up to a corner of the room, and everyone involuntarily turns to look.

"You're being silly," Barbara says, trying to draw the squirming child to her. The others chuckle and whisper, smiling at her misunderstanding. But Genevieve thinks it would be typical of Dad to try and startle everyone.

As soon as she can, Genevieve slips downstairs to her father's workshop. The bumper sticker on the doorframe reads, "I'm not a dirty old man, I'm just a sexy senior citizen." He used to bring home car loads of antique furniture and junk which he would repair and refinish. The box of trinkets on the work table must have come from his last auction. Fifty cents, he likely bid for it, just for the sake of bringing something home. Christa and Genevieve used to fight over these, but as they got older it became more difficult to pick out anything of interest. Their father would hover, eager to see them choose. Genevieve pocketed all sorts of junk to satisfy him.

A loud creak startles the adrenaline through her numb limbs. The door to the workshop opens, slowly, tentatively, and there is no one there, it seems, until she looks down. Samantha.

"What are you doing?" the child asks.

"Looking at my dad's stuff."

"Is he here?"

Genevieve looks around. The smell of this room, the varnish, the sawdust, so much embodies her father that he could be present, if she were to ask her nose. He was here less than twenty-four hours ago. The room and tools still expect him. "Do you see him?"

Samantha merely shrugs and climbs up on a chair to inspect the box of trinkets. "What are all these?" she asks, with wonder and hope of acquisition.

"My dad got them at an auction."

Samantha sorts through the box with her nearly transparent fingers. A couple of items catch her fancy, a keychain and an empty jewelry case.

"Anything you'd like?" Genevieve asks.

Tess calls from the top of the basement steps, "Genevieve! Come up, the ministers are here."

Genevieve walks behind Samantha who parades her treasures into the living room. "Look what Uncle Gordon gave me!" she announces.

There are two ministers in the room, the younger, controversially, a woman. Genevieve's father expressed a particular wish to have this woman conduct his funeral ceremony. "Rather sit and stare at her for an hour than old MacGregor," he used to say. He made no secret of the reason for his renewed enthusiasm for church attendance in the past few years.

Reverend Joan Blackstone is chubby and bright on the couch beside older Reverend MacGregor. This is the woman Genevieve's parents tried to set up as her counselor after one of her hospital stays two years ago. Back then, Genevieve shuffled in to Reverend Joan's study for their first meeting, in clothes far too big. She had lost weight since the night Gary left her in the emergency room.

"Hello, Genevieve. I'm Joan. Do you know why you're here?"

"On earth?" Genevieve asked, and laughed loudly, aware that her sense of humour was out of whack with the rest of humankind. Like everything else. But Joan laughed.

"Sure. Why are you on earth?" she asked.

"To torment my parents."

"They must have done something terrible in a previous life," Joan mused and Genevieve smiled. It was already clear why her father found this woman charming. "Your father wanted us to meet, so let me start by telling you about myself," Joan said and proceeded to describe her background, her family, and how she came to be ordained. When she finished, Genevieve smiled.

"Now I know why my father sent me here," she said.

"Because I'm a minister?" Joan asked.

"No. Because you've got a man, a couple of kids and a good, round bottom."

Joan looked startled. "That may be," she said. She continued asking Genevieve about herself and attempted to give her advice, but there was a strain through the rest of the interview. They were both relieved when Genevieve left.

Reverend Joan looks kindly on Genevieve now, laying a quick arm across her shoulders. When Reverend MacGregor begins his condolence speech, Genevieve quickly drifts away. She is surprised by the calm way she is beginning to feel, the quietness. So unlike that day four years ago when Dad had his first heart attack. She had been living with Gary on the west coast for several months, and her parents were pleased. "Children would give you reason to be this happy forever," her father said. "Why don't you marry this Gary?" Genevieve was tempted to ask whether his children made him happy.

Her mother backed him up, describing Barbara's glowing pregnancy. "It puts everything in perspective, Gen." They had been desperately courting Scott and Barbara's coming children for fear of missing out on grandchildren of their own. Then came this ray of hope, which Genevieve quickly dashed.

"I don't think I want any children," she said. A week later, her father had his first heart attack and Genevieve knew it was her fault. Gary did not recognize the woman who returned after a week at home, visiting her father in the hospital. Genevieve had been out west for two years before she met Gary. They were gentle years, during which she feigned a fortitude she hoped would become hers through habit. If she ever mentioned her past difficulties to Gary, he assumed she had outgrown them. But after the heart attack, it was as though she had shrunk.

For the first time, Genevieve told him that she had attempted suicide several years earlier, and Gary recognized the veiled threat. When she took too many sleeping pills with some wine, he acted quickly, leaving her alone in the hospital emergency room. He cleared his stuff from the apartment, and she never saw him again.

"You don't want to get up in front of everyone, do you, Gen?" her mother is saying as she snaps to.

Everyone else's face is a question, but her mother's is a frown. She does not know what her mother is asking, but she senses how she must answer. "No," Gen says.

"I think Scott should deliver the eulogy," her mother continues quickly.

*

After supper, Genevieve helps Tess with the dishes. "You know, if you want to speak at the funeral, you should," Tess says quietly. "Don't let anyone make you feel like you shouldn't. Even your mother."

Genevieve looks up at Tess's tall dark head with surprise. "No. It would be too awkward."

"Why? I'd like to hear you," Tess says. Genevieve feels a flood of gratitude, but is tongue-tied. She really does like Tess a great deal.

On her way to her old downstairs bedroom, Genevieve glimpses the teary good-night between Christa and Tess, who is leaving for the motel. Genevieve feels a surge of loneliness at the sight, and keeps descending. She would like to fall asleep quickly, safely, but the atmosphere rings with disturbances. It reminds Genevieve of the drafty old mansion which housed the first group-home she inhabited. She had come home from university, her vision tunneled with darkness, and not even Christa could pull her out of it. After weeks of trying to cope with their dingy prodigal, Genevieve's parents drove her to that big house on the hill where wraith-like girls shuddered through the halls. The look of pained confusion on her father's face after he had poked her and said good-bye beat itself into her brain. Then Genevieve was handed over to a straight and severe housemother, and put to bed in a cardboard-coloured room.

Just as she begins to doze, Genevieve has a strong but fleeting experience of her father's presence and her eyes fly open. It is as if she has seen his face, chuckling like he did after a lewd joke. "What are you hanging around here for?" Genevieve whispers. She imagines his reunion with those whose names he had heard over the radio at noon. He would make his way among the women, patting and charming. Angels or not, they are still women.

*

By the time she comes upstairs for breakfast, the house is full again with mourners. "Gen, come have some coffee," Tess says, passing her a cup. The group is strangely quiet. Scott and Christa are pouring over a mound of papers.

They have been discussing me, Genevieve thinks.

Scott clears his throat. "Really, there's nothing to worry about, Aunt Lily. There's your pension, and Gordon made arrangements for . . . everything you need."

Genevieve's toast turns to felt in her mouth. Her mother is worried about how she will continue to support her daughter at the costly private group-home. I am thirty-four years old, and more worry than comfort to my mother even one day after his death, she thinks, and believes the gatherers must think the same. Taking her coffee, she leaves with Samantha who is clamouring for someone to play a game with her, but not without catching Christa's eye.

Poor Christa. Her tired face this morning so contrasts her fiery look that day several years ago. Her father had just finished another one of his tales, this one about a new waitress at the local restaurant, how he had broken her in with a great big tip and a pat on the behind. "For good measure," he had told her, "and you certainly measure up, as far as I can see!"

"I don't know why we let you get away with this!" Christa said. She looked ready to explode.

He waved her away. "Never knew a woman didn't like a compliment."

"How can you think that's a compliment?"

"She smiled well enough. Just being friendly."

Christa rubbed her face in exasperation. "You should not assume you know what will make us happy."

"I don't know what makes you so unhappy," he gestured towards Genevieve. "Look at Genny. Why couldn't a husband and kids make her happy?" he asked, then added with a grin, "A little warmth in her bed would put some flesh on her bones."

Christa sighed. "One of these days, you're going to squeeze the wrong bum." This made her father laugh heartily.

Samantha lays out the cards of her memory game with

intense concentration, then instructs Genevieve to begin. Genevieve turns over a picture of a grinning, clown-like man.

"Huh," Samantha says. "Looks like Uncle Gordon when he sticks his teeth out."

Genevieve's father already had a set of false teeth by the time his children were born. He loved to scare them by shoving the teeth out in a grotesque grin. With Samantha, his great-niece, the tradition continued. Genevieve still sees those teeth in her dreams and even now a vivid picture of her father's face flits across the insides of her eyes. She reaches across the spread of memory cards and turns one randomly. A match.

Samantha looks up with wide uncanny eyes. "You're good at this game."

She reminds Genevieve of Christa, who always begged her to play a game when it was raining outside. Things would begin well and Genevieve would be excited, but eventually the darkness and frustration would ebb into her vision. Christa would see the downturning sides of her mouth and offer concessions.

"It's okay. You can land on my Boardwalk without paying this time. You can be a guest," she would say. It was not because Genevieve was unskilled or slow. It was the devastation of chance which threw her. A bad-luck toss of the dice could tip Genevieve once again into the quicksand. Eventually, Christa stopped asking her to play.

On her second night in the basement, Genevieve waits in the dark. What would the ghost of a seventy-five-year-old man, a self-proclaimed sexy senior citizen look like? It is hard to imagine his heavy lumpen shape fluttering in the air with hummingbird wings. Perhaps she would just see that protruding false-teeth grin like the Cheshire cat, or feel a big-fingered poke to the ribs. He would never agree to stick around in that wheezing body, she thinks. He would be off looking for the best deal on something young and nubile, perfect. Genevieve sighs and climbs under the covers.

*

The funeral morning sends a Juney shaft of light through the dust and snow-marked basement window. Her father never got around to cleaning them this spring. There is movement upstairs, but Genevieve lies still, staring around the achingly familiar room. There are still mementos tucked into corners. At the edge of the mirror is a snapshot of Christa and Genevieve when they were toddlers. Genevieve is behind, tagging along. "You and your shadow," their parents used to call whenever Christa passed by with smaller Genny in tow, and in the black-and-white photograph, the analogy is striking. In strictly physical terms, Christa and Genevieve resemble each other. But Genevieve's blonde hair darkened gradually to a dirtyish brown, while Christa's remained sunny. Even at three, the downpull on Genevieve's facial muscles is there, creating dips below her eyes and in her cheeks that would later become caverns. Genevieve remembers how Christa fascinated her, how the thought of clinging like a shadow pleased her. She did not know that shadows disappear in the dark. She climbs out of bed and puts on one of the loose, dark print dresses that her father hated. "You look like Laura Ingalls," he would say.

The funeral service is crowded and conventional, despite the woman minister. Scott does not mention babysitter hugs in his eulogy. Afterwards, the luncheon at the house spills out to the backyard. Genevieve feels choked by the moist clasping hands and staring eyes. "I'm feeling claustrophobic," she tells Christa, who looks smudged herself.

Tess hears her. "Let's see if we can get out for a walk. Just us," she says.

Christa brightens. "By the lake. We can drive over."

As they plan their escape, Samantha approaches with her memory game. "I can't play now," Genevieve says. "We're going out for a walk."

"Can I come?" Samantha asks.

Genevieve shrugs. "Ask your mom."

Barbara looks from Genevieve to Christa and Tess, then back again with unease. But Scott nods in Barbara's direction.

Genevieve buckles Samantha carefully into the back seat of Tess's car and climbs in beside. They arrive at the same beach where the family once picnicked, but this time it is deserted. Genevieve carries Samantha's shoes and socks so she can walk barefoot in the sand. The top is hot, reflecting the sun, but the cool and damp is only a paper thin layer below.

"Can I dig?" Samantha asks, crouching down in the sand with a couple of tool-like twigs. Genevieve lowers herself to a dry patch beside her. The murmur of Christa's voice fades as she and Tess saunter down the beach, hands held. Genevieve experiences an exquisite moment of loneliness watching them, while the lake wind blows through the wisps around her face.

"Let's play bury," Samantha says, showing Genevieve a piece of driftwood she's picked up. "This can be the box."

"It's called a coffin," Genevieve says.

"Coffin," Samantha repeats. "Was Uncle Gordon inside that box?" she asks. Genevieve nods.

Samantha digs a vaguely rectangular slot in the sand and sets the driftwood beside. She bows her head and clasps her hands together. "God is great, God is good, Let us thank him for our food, Amen," she recites. She puts the wood in the hole and covers it up, patting the sand down flat. "When does he get to come out?"

Genevieve shrugs.

Samantha stares at the grave, then begins furiously digging it up. When she pulls out the wood, she tosses it over her shoulder into the lake, shrieking with laughter. Genevieve smiles at her face of delight. "He's swimming," Genevieve says.

"He's swimming!" Samantha hollers, and jumps up and down, tossing sand into the wind. "There he is!"

She and Genevieve stand waving wildly out to the horizon. Far down along a curve in the beach, Christa and Tess wave back.

"Let's catch up," Samantha says, and takes Genevieve's hand to run down the sand.

Achevé d'imprimer
en septembre deux mille quatre, sur les presses
de l'imprimerie Gauvin, Gatineau, Québec